SCOTT A. SIMON

KATHERINE'S CROSS

* * *

DREAMFIELD MEDIA WORKS
STOCKTON, NEW JERSEY

*For Claire and Norma
With Love & Affection*

*To Peek, wherever you are. Your stories
of our Irish roots, the mines, the mills
and riding a black stallion naked
though the streets of Bristol serve
to remind me life should be fun.*

*Special thanks to Brian, Shelly, Aida, MJ,
Barb, Shane, Dodhi, Gayle, Doc Tindall,
Kate, Nancy, Renie, Robb and Christine.*

I am what I am, Leila, and if there are self-made purgatories, then we all have to live in them. Mine can be no worse than someone else's.

Mr. Spock

THE BEGINNING: August 1945

One hundred feet shy of the entrance, a man crouched near a chain link fence. Obscured by smog that settled like an acidic mist, he waited until the morning shift passed through the security gate. When the last ID was checked, he made his move.

"Where do you think you're going?" the guard said. With a flick of the switch, his flashlight illuminated the stranger's face. "A little lost, aren't you?"

"I'm not lost," the man said, shielding his eyes. "I've lived here my whole life, I'm here to work." He pulled a wrinkled letter from his shirt pocket.

"Work at the steel mill? You? A Negro?" The guard took the paper. When he finished reading he pushed back his cap, and directed the light toward the ground. "So, you're Gerald Davis the war hero."

Gerald nodded, offering his hand.

"Well, I'll be," the guard continued and gave Gerald a hearty handshake. "I've heard a lot about you. I'm John O'Hara. I'm fresh from the army myself." He steered the conversation back to the letter. "This notice says you're to report to the maintenance shed." He pointed into the haze. "Here's what you do, buddy. Follow the gravel for a half-mile. You'll come to a metal shack. There'll be a few other guys hanging around. You can't miss it."

"Thanks, Officer O'Hara."

"Not a problem, lad. I'd do anything to help a fellow GI. Good luck."

Gerald walked the stone path, thoughts of opportunity scrolled through his head. When he passed the machine shop, dreams of someday being foreman accented his stride. At the motor pool that bubble burst, pricked by the hateful stares of men gathered around a pile of worn truck tires. He felt eyes zero in on his back. Hair on his neck bristled, but after an over-the-shoulder glance, relieved that nobody followed, he moved on.

Loose rocks crunched under his feet, each step closing the gap between him and the uncertain. Where the hell is this thing, he thought, straining to see through the man-made fog. One hundred yards later the outline of a shack came in to view. When he arrived at the maintenance shed a man dressed in a soiled, white jumpsuit blocked his path. "Whoa, boy," he said in a puff of whiskey-breath. "Where do ya think you're going?" He smacked his dirty palm on Gerald's work shirt. Gerald brushed the gesture away and took hold of the door.

"Ya don't hear too well, do ya, Sambo? I asked ya a question." The man grabbed him from behind. Gerald spun around so fast that their lips almost touched.

"I don't know your name," he said. "But watch who you're calling 'Sambo.' "

"Listen, spook. Kelly's the name. It's Bob Kelly. And I'll call ya whatever the hell I want."

* * *

Gerald Davis, the first Black man hired by Battle Hymn Steel, shoveled, swept, gardened, and tolerated Kelly's insults.

"The only reason they hired ya is that Silver Star. Hell, ya probably stole it just like every other goddamn thing ya have."

The torment even followed Gerald into the latrine, but he had survived the Nazis, and he wasn't about to let, what he considered to be, some white punk run him off.

Kelly's harassment continued throughout the week, but Gerald remained calm. His father told him the trouble would eventually go away.

* * *

One night in the old part of town, after dinner in the apartment Gerald shared with his parents above the family's grocery store, he smacked the table with his palm.

"I could kill that guy, Dad."

"What will that get you? The electric chair?"

"I don't mean kill him kill him." Gerald stood, slamming his hand against the wall.

"I know you don't, son. But I bet it'd feel good to bust him up a little." Tom sat back and smiled.

"It sure would." Gerald shadow-boxed the wall.

"That'd be easy for you, and that's just what those fools want you to do."

"What fools?" He threw a left at his bobbing silhouette followed by an uppercut. "What are you talkin' about?"

"Son, there's fools who wanna see a Black man fall on his face, who wanna say 'those Negroes ain't worth nothin'. They don't deserve a chance.' Those are the fools I'm talkin' 'bout."

Gerald stopped and bit his lower lip. "I didn't think of it that way."

"Heck, what normal young man would? I'm tellin' you, son. The best thing is to let it blow over. Idiots like that get tired. Sooner or later they move on."

Mrs. Davis cleared the table as Toby, their little dog, tagged along for scraps. Tom lit a cigar while Gerald contemplated fatherly advice.

A truck roared down the street, bringing Tom and Gerald to the front window. They watched as the jalopy skidded to a halt in front of the store. The horn honked accompanied by repeated shouts of " Special Delivery." Then there was a loud thump. A flaming bag of cow manure landed on the front porch.

"Fire! Fire!" Tom yelled.

"I'll get the bucket, Dad!"

They ran down the stairs. In a panic, they doused the flames with five gallons of sand. "That was a close one," Gerald said.

"This place would go up like kindlin'." Tom struggled to catch his breath, wiping sweat from his brow.

Neighbors across the street peered through drawn curtains.

"What the hell are you looking at?" Gerald screamed.

"Don't pay attention to them. Let it blow over, son."

Gerald kicked the smoldering sack and followed his father back to the apartment.

* * *

The next day at the mill, more insults and physical threats ensued. It'll blow over, Gerald thought and continued his work. Later that afternoon Kelly and two like-minded friends were supposed to help plant flowers, but instead they lounged on the cool grass, sharing swigs from a pint bottle.

Gerald had just finished a new hole and turned to grab a bunch of pansies. Kelly stood over him, zipper down, about to urinate. His hips gyrated like a strip-tease dancer. Gerald sprang up and stepped away.

"What's wrong, boy? Never seen a real man before?"

Gerald averted his eyes.

"Don't turn your head on this thing, boy. Your momma didn't."

With one bone-shattering punch, Gerald knocked Kelly to the ground, out cold. His buddies ran for their lives. Kelly earned a trip to Battle Hymn General Hospital where he remained for three days, his jaw wired tight, unable to speak or eat. While recovering, he wrote a note to the mill's maintenance foreman saying, *I tripped and fell on my shovel.* That settled the matter.

* * *

The same day Kelly was discharged, Gerald came home exhausted. He had been loading carts with heavy stone, but he was happy. The work felt as therapeutic as shutting Kelly's mouth. With two restful nights of sleep under his belt, he looked forward to making it three in a row. He opened a window, summer nights in the valley being as hot as the days. Toby slept at the foot of the bed while Tom and Carol snored in the next room. Gerald relaxed into his pillow, and his eyelids closed.

An hour later, in front of the store, truck motors revved, air-horns blasted, and the flames exploded. But this time it was Molotov cocktails. When those gasoline bombs crashed through the display window, a wood-hungry fire began to devour the store.

Gerald almost stumbled as he ran and shoved one leg into his boxers. He and his parents, dressed in nothing but bathrobes, hurried down the stairs to the street. A fireball rose into the night. Gerald quaked with anger. Carol wept in Tom's arms, their store engulfed. She lifted her head.

"Toby! My God! Toby's in there!"

Everything happened so fast that neither Tom nor Carol could react to Gerald's charge up the stairs and into the apartment. They stood paralyzed as their son moved through the flames, the dog squealing. Tom jumped into action.

"Son. Son. Come outta there," he yelled as he ran toward the building.

The roar of the fire grew. Tom's attempt to climb the stairs failed, heat forcing him to the street. Carol stood with her mouth wide open. Her body trembled. One hundred-year-old timbers snapped like bones, and the roof collapsed.

"Help me! Help me!" Gerald's scream rose over the sound of the imploding structure as he fell to the first floor, consumed by flames.

Carol's arms shot into the air. "Jesus! Oh, Jesus! Not my little baby."

She made a break for the store, but Tom grabbed her around the waist. She wailed and slumped to her knees. "Lord, what have you done?"

Gerald howled, but eventually there was no sound except for crackling embers, canned food exploding, and Carol's screams.

* * *

The next day, city investigators picked through the rubble, but found nothing. "This thing was so damn hot," they said, "we only have the boy's teeth and bones to work with." Their conclusion: faulty wiring.

After their son's funeral, Tom and Carol returned to the old part of town. They stared at their home, a heap of charred wood and brick. A young man who owned the corner hardware store rested his hand on Tom's shoulder. "We'll help you rebuild, Mr. Davis," he said.

Tom gazed at his neighbor.

"Son," he said. "There's nothin' left to rebuild. It's all over for us – Carol and me. That boy was all we had in this world."

Carol cried, "Why, Jesus? Why did you let this happen?"

Tom wrapped his arm around her, helping her to the family car. They said good riddance to Battle Hymn, Pennsylvania. Where they went? Down South, some people said, but nobody actually knew and nobody cared.

1.

Katherine O'Hara expected great things to drop into her lap after she graduated Saint Ann's Catholic Academy. But by February of 1963 her schoolgirl enthusiasm had eroded to dull reality. She lived with her parents, attended church on Sunday, cooked dinner on Tuesday and Thursday, ironed clothes on Wednesday, and mopped floors Monday and Friday. Saturdays at Gerber's soda fountain were the only fun times, but fewer of her girlfriends attended, many of them married-off during the previous summer and fall. She pondered this as she stood before the crucifix fastened to the wall above her bed. After blessing herself she went to the front porch, took a deep breath and started down the street.

Generations of Irish women before her had lived their lives behind a lonely barrier of self-denial; their needs were the needs of the family. Katherine wanted no part of it. Instead, dressed in her best wool jumper, knee socks, penny loafers and navy pea coat, she walked along Lower Wood Street - a side road populated by row houses built sixty years earlier. She had told her parents she was going to meet a boy for breakfast. She skipped over the part about his being a Protestant named Ron Kelly.

Her saunter brought her to Division Avenue. She crossed onto Upper Wood Street. A fickle breeze swished her golden bangs from one eye to the other. When she neared the middle of the block, the mill's 8:00 a.m. whistle sounded the start of another Saturday morning shift. Two houses down, a wood shingle swung on brass hooks, the name *Kelly* hacked into its unpainted surface.

She wasn't supposed to meet Ron until 8:30, but she decided to surprise him. After climbing four steps, and covering ten feet of cracked walkway, she stood on the Kelly's porch – a ramshackle of empty beer bottles, barren flowerpots, and a tarp-covered divan. She tapped on one of the front door's diamond-shaped windows. A man's voice responded. "Ya son of a bitch." He kicked the door. It opened a few inches. "Yeah?"

"I'm...I'm here to see Ron."

"Who are ya?" He rubbed his squinted eyes.

"Katherine O'Hara. I live a mile down the road at the end of street."

"Lower Wood Street?" His voice woke up. "And ya here for a date with my boy?"

"Yes. Is he in?"

He opened the door and closed his robe, covering his fuzzy chest.

"Yeah. Come in. Ron'll be back in a minute. He's returnin' a cup of flour his mother borrowed."

She crossed the threshold, entering a room of drawn drapes, one chair and a couch bordered by unpainted end tables, each with a lamp not lit.

"Gimme ya coat," he said.

"You're Ron's father?"

He hung her coat on a hook and bolted the door.

"Yeah, I'm Bob Kelly." He extended his arm toward the couch. "Have a seat."

Katherine's eyes adjusted to the low-lit environment one step at a time. Her nose wrestled stale alcohol and body odor.

"Go on," he said. "It don't bite."

She baby-stepped for fear of tripping. As she neared the couch, his hand came out of the dark and clamped her mouth; his forearm completed the chokehold. She struggled, a funk oozing from his every pore, his sandpaper face pressed to her ear.

"Listen, ya little Catholic tramp. Ya lookin' for a little fun? Wanna date a Protestant? This is what happens when ya fuck around with my people."

She thrashed and fought until he directed her eyes to a buck knife on one of the end tables.

"I'm going to loosen my grip. If ya make a goddamn peep, I'll gut ya like a pig. Got it?"

Her eyes widened.

"Ya got it?"

The more she fought, the more his grip tightened. Faced with suffocation, she nodded, and he released. Instantly, a scream rose from her.

He took her by the hair, shoving her face to the blade. "Ya don't think I'll do it? Try me."

Katherine, subdued, stood with her chin pressed to her chest.

"Are ya gonna keep that trap shut?" He yanked on her hair. She managed a small nod.

"Look at me," he said, taking a handful of her cheek. "Off with that dress."

Her eyes darted as if there were someone else in the room. He slapped her. "I said off with that goddamn dress."

He re-directed her to the knife. She slipped from her jumper. It fell to the floor, gathered at her ankles.

"Them shoes, too."

She stepped from her loafers.

"Now them bra and panties."

She froze.

He smacked his lips and grabbed the knife.

She was nude, all but for her socks.

He slipped from his robe and moved toward her. Katherine backed away until the couch became a last stand. He snagged her by the neck and sat on the thread-worn sofa.

"Straddle me."

She heard the words but didn't understand. He smacked her. His nails dug into her hips. She fought his two hundred fifty pounds until her thighs ached, but he was too much. He kicked her legs apart. She twisted and squirmed. He flung her arms over his shoulders and onto the back of the couch. Photos of a family from some distant past hung on the wall two inches from her face.

"Do as I say." His hand fumbled between her legs.

"Don't. No. Don't do it," she pleaded."

He explored until he hit his mark.

"Oh no. For the love of God, don't do it," she cried.

The first jab sent wheels of pain rolling through her abdomen and down her arms.

"Got ya, ya little whore."

Blood trickled down her thighs, his putrid breath invading her nose. He raised himself until their pubic bones met. The assault continued until he put the knife to her throat.

"I'm too old for this shit. Ya do the work."

"Oh, Jesus," she whispered. "Kill me now."

He grunted, gnawing her breasts as his free hand guided her motion. After what seemed an eternity, his body stiffened. She felt his jolt inside her.

For lack of any other support, she wept into his hairy shoulder. He heaved and cast her aside.

Kelly swiped his groin with a tee shirt then tossed it to Katherine.

"Get the blood off them legs, and get dressed."

When she finished, thoughts of being stabbed to death, rolled in a carpet, and dumped into the Battle Hymn trash pit seemed like a reprieve. But as he displayed the knife she swallowed hard, expecting cold steel to cut her throat. His lips brushed her ear.

"If ya tell anybody about what happened, and that includes my boy," he whispered, "I'll find ya and cut ya and I won't stop there." He took her by the chin, squeezing until her mouth popped open. "It'll be ya pig mother who get's it next. When I'm done, I'll kill her and ya company-cop father." He twisted her hair and dragged her to the door. "Remember. Not a word or ya family's dead meat."

Before she could react, he shoved her out.

She stood on the porch, coat in hand, as smokestacks spewed familiar waste. A few cars passed by. She didn't remember walking to the sidewalk.

God, why didn't you let him kill me?

She wandered. Somewhere downtown the cold penetrated her flesh. His foul smell hovered over everything as she donned her coat.

I can't go home. Not yet. They'll know.

His remnants began to seep from her. She went to Woolworth's, purchased a fresh pair of underwear and hurried to Gerber's - the only private bathroom nearby. As she approached the drugstore, she saw Ron in a cheap leather jacket leaning against the plate glass, son of the devil. "There you are," he said. "I thought you chickened out."

* * *

Throughout the week, she struggled to appear normal, fearing for her parents' lives. As part of the cover-up, she went to Gerber's and laughed phony laughs. She even chatted it up with Ron Kelly, hoping her subtle advances would somehow be communicated to his father, convincing him that she had put the hellish event behind her. But after four weeks of fraud and a missed menstrual cycle, she had to face reality. The first wave of nausea hit her on a Friday night.

The next day as she neared Division Avenue, her skin crawled, her body shivered. She turned off of Wood Street and headed east. Saint Ann's Church sat on the corner three blocks down. It was late in the afternoon, confession drawing to a close. Inside the one hundred-year-old edifice, built for the glory of God on the backs of blue-collar donations, Katherine knelt in a pew toward the rear. She wanted to ensure that she would be the last sinner of the day to seek redemption.

Her hands covered her face and she pretended to pray. Every so often she peeked at two burgundy-draped doorways along the wall. Hidden from view by an ornate wooden door, Father Ryan sat on a bench between the spaces, while parishioners came and went to his left and right.

Mrs. McKeon stepped from behind one of the plush drapes, made the sign of the cross, and walked to the altar to complete her penance. Peter Downs, grandfather of Joe Downs - a boy who had eyes for Katherine – took her place. Two minutes later, Jenny Purdy came from behind drape number two. Not proceeding to the altar, she walked down the aisle and out the front door, Mrs. McKeon not far behind. Katherine approached the confessional; grandfather Downs was mumbling to the priest about using foul language. She ducked behind the curtain, knelt on the hardwood kneeler, folded her hands and waited in the dark, trying not to eavesdrop on Mr. Downs' confession. There was a moment of silence then she heard Father Ryan recite the prayer of absolution.

Dominus noster Jesus Christus te absolvat; et ego auctoritate ipsius te absolvo ab omni vinculo excommunicationis et interdicti in quantum possum et tu indiges. Deinde, ego te absolvo a peccatis tuis in nomine Patris, et Filii, et Spiritus Sancti. Amen.

With that, all was forgiven. Old Mr. Downs had a clean slate for another week. She listened to his footsteps fade. The window opened. A faint light seeped through the sheer fabric to outline Father Ryan's jowly face. She blessed herself and prayed, "Oh my God I am sorry for having offended thee." But before she could finish the priest interrupted.

"Katherine O'Hara," he said. "Why haven't you been to confession in the past month? Don't you want to save your soul?"

"Yes," she whispered.

"Then I suggest you get back on schedule or you'll be on your way to hell."

"That's why I'm here, Father. I've been part of a big sin...a mortal sin, and I'm trapped."

As her eyes adjusted, she saw the priest put his index finger against his cheek.

"Tell me about your sin, child."

"I'm pregnant."

He sighed and stiffened his posture. "Which of the boys was it?"

She stammered. "I...I..."

"Tell me, girl or you'll be damned."

"He wasn't a Catholic. He was a Protestant." Now her tears flowed freely.

"I don't want to hear any more," the priest said. "Not only have you committed sin, you've blackened your soul by fornicating with someone outside our faith."

"I did't ask for this baby," she moaned. "I don't want it."

"Listen to me. If you end the life you're carrying, there'll be no saving you from eternal damnation, and you'll go to prison."

Bob Kelly's warning replayed in her head, *Not a word or your family's dead meat.*

"What should I do? Tell me what God wants."

"You'll have this baby and beg His forgiveness."

Father Ryan gave her absolution, provided she did as he said. The cloth divider slammed shut. She sobbed down the steps and onto the sidewalk. On the way home, several scenarios played out in her head: reveal the crime and her parents die, have an abortion and her soul dies, or create a new truth and live a lie.

2.

The first of spring brought buds to trees, daffodils to thawed soil, and life to Katherine's plan. In the back bedroom of her family's end-cap row house – the only space that provided true privacy, no common wall, no neighbors with ears pressed to tumblers pinned to the plaster – she sat on the corner of her mother and father's bed.

The black revolver felt heavier than she imagined. She spun the chamber. The zipping reminded her of the wheel-of-fortune game at Saint Ann's church bazaar. The coolness of metal hit her skin as she ran her finger along the barrel and rubbed her thumb over the hammer's beveled edges. The sweet smell of gun oil dashed toward her nose as she lifted the weapon to eye level. A black leather holster streaked with brown cracks lay beside her. Sixteen .38 caliber bullets hung in the cartridge loops.

"Katherine, stop playing with that thing. It's not a toy. Put it in the holster and pass it to me, like a good girl." Mr. O' Hara's voice was a murmur as he examined the gold badge on the front of his cap.

"What's the big deal? I'm just looking at it," she said, passing the holstered weapon.

He placed the cap on his head as if it were a crown. She watched as he stood in front of a dressing mirror, admiring the sharp creases of his gray pants and starched perfection of the matching shirt. He pushed down on the fluffy epaulettes and, as usual, they rebounded when he removed his fingers.

"Perfect ironing job," he said.

"Thanks, Daddy," she mumbled, fluffing pillows.

For her, except for handling the pistol, it was the same old routine. He swung the gun belt around his waist then fastened the gold buckle. From atop an oak dresser, he plucked a badge with the words "Battle Hymn Steel" etched in blue on its gold-plated surface and fastened it to his left breast pocket.

"Daddy, why don't you keep bullets in your gun?"

Puzzled, O'Hara turned his head. "Now what kind of question is that?"

"Well, it seems useless to have a gun without bullets. Why don't you load it?"

"That's none of your business."

Hurt grew on Katherine's face.

"I'm sorry, sweetheart," he said. "I didn't mean to sound rude."

Katherine offered a joyless smile as she folded the night quilt. Mrs. O'Hara came into the room. "Aren't you going to tell your father the good news?" she said.

Katherine froze.

"Now what secrets are you girls keeping," he asked as he gave his image the once-over in the mirror. Katherine moved to his side.

"I know this'll be a bit of a shock," she said.

"Now what can you say that'd shock me?"

Katherine braced her body against the dresser. "I'm getting married."

He looked into her moist green eyes, pushed his cap back, and grasped her arms. Katherine felt a splash of joy as the broad smile spread across his ruddy face. Then the cheer faded. "What kind of surprise is this," he said, looking to his wife. "You've been going around with someone behind our backs? What are you hiding?"

Katherine sat on the bed. "I'm not hiding anything."

"Don't lie to me," he said then his expression softened. "I'm sorry. There I go again. Shooting my mouth off. Let's start over."

At that moment, she felt nothing but the deepest love for her father.

"You were afraid we wouldn't approve, weren't you?" Katherine chewed on her lip.

"Is it that handsome Riley boy who sits with his family at Sunday Mass?" O'Hara cocked his head and thrust his jaw. "I've seen the eyes that boy gives you. It's a father's job."

She said nothing, but felt a jab of pain realizing that she would never live the life her father proposed.

Perplexed, O'Hara massaged his chin.

"Not the Riley boy, eh? Let's see. The Downs chap? Now there's a good one. Works in the accounting office, not the hearth. A good future with him."

She sat on the edge of the bed. Her father's six-foot frame towered over her with a policemen's authority. She was about to speak when he snapped his fingers.

"I've got it," he said. Her heart sank. His eyes twinkled. She almost began to cry when he looked skyward and begged, "Lord, help me if I'm right."

He knelt at his daughter's feet like a penitent. "Please, say it isn't the McGowan boy. He's a handsome lad, but his brain's a lump of coal. He'll work barges till his back gives way."

Katherine crossed the room then turned to look at her father's humbled image. "It's none of those boys."

"Then who is he? Someone new in the church or from another town?"

"He's from Battle Hymn." The next words exploded a rotten taste in her mouth. "His father operates the crane at the mill."

O'Hara's eyes hardened. "Works the crane? The crane!" His voice rolled full-throated. "You mean Ronald Kelly? If you marry into that Protestant family you'll condemn your soul to hell, and your children will be bastards in the eyes of the Church!"

"Maybe in the eyes of the Church, but not in the eyes of God," she replied, feigning ill temper. "I'm eighteen. I'm marrying Ronald Kelly, and that's final."

"How could you do it to me, to your poor mother?" he pleaded. "The boy's not a Catholic." His voice searched for reasoning. "We had you baptized, sent you to Saint Ann's and paid through the nose for your tuition. We saw that you took the Sacraments. The bishop traveled from Philadelphia for your Confirmation. He presided over your official entry to our Faith and now you'll throw that away?"

Her heart ached, but her face revealed nothing.

He stood, spun on his heel, and went to the kitchen. Katherine wanted to run and tell him the truth, but instead, she listened to the refrigerator open then close. There were a few more stomps before the front door squeaked once and slammed shut.

3.

Bob Kelly pushed up from the kitchen table. His face exploded in anger, fingers raking unwashed hair. "Ya'll never marry a Papist. Do ya hear me? Never. Ya idiot."

Ron lit a cigarette and smirked. Kelly went to his wife's side. She slouched over a sink cluttered with egg-stained dishes and an iron skillet drenched in bacon grease.

"Did ya hear that, Margret? Our boy wants to marry a Catholic, a Catholic," he snorted. "And *her* of all people. It's an insult to our heritage. Ya must be out of your goddamn mind. Between them and the jungle bunnies, our people been losin' work at the mill left and right." He paced the ten by ten kitchen, lighting a Lucky Strike and pulling a deep drag. His punctuated exhale sent a bluish tube of smoke to the front of the house. His heavy look fell on his wife. He collected a metal lunchbox from the refrigerator. "Try and talk some sense into this son of mine, will ya?" After giving her a harsh peck, he stormed through the hanging cloud and out the front door. The thuds bounced family pictures from the living room wall onto the worn-out couch.

Ron went to his mother. Tears budded from the corners of her eyes. Her red hair hung in wisps from the metal clip fastened to the collapsed bun atop her head. She turned to Ron.

"Your father's just a man. You know that, don't you, Ronnie?"

He puffed his cigarette, not wanting to interrupt her rare moment of self-expression.

"He's just blowin' off steam. He doesn't mean to hurt you. He's just acting the way he was taught," she said.

"What do you mean?"

"I've tried to shield you from the hate, son, but you know it's been goin' on for generations. If your father knew how I really felt about it, he'd strangle me." She grabbed a dishrag and twisted until it drew out to a narrow strip of rope-like cloth. "The past has its hooks in him and I don't know how to yank 'em out."

She turned to face him, probing the openness of his James Dean looks in the way only a mother can – behind the kindness of his eyes, underneath youthful waves of hair, around his soft expression, and down into his heart.

"You're not like your father, are you, son?" she said. "I wouldn't want you to jump into his mess."

"Ma, don't worry. Whatever makes him hate anybody who isn't one of us isn't part of me."

Her eyes brightened.

"I don't hate anybody," he said. "Besides, this is my business. I'm eighteen and Katherine O'Hara's marrying me, not him."

She pushed water drops from the sides of her face then placed her palms on the square of his chin. Ron kissed her cheek and the salty tears ran over his lips.

"Don't worry," he assured, pulling his lunch box from the refrigerator. "It'll be okay."

The clatter of dishwashing filled the kitchen. Ron savored a puff from his dying cigarette. He looked at the clock, gave his mother another kiss, and hurried out the front door, trying to arrive at the steel mill before the 8:00 a.m. whistle.

He paused on the front porch as a giant wind kicked up red ash that draped the neighborhood. He secured the lunchbox under his arm, crushed the glowing cigarette between his fingertips and flicked the remains to the dormant grass. He shielded his eyes and sprinted through dust devils of iron ore, following his father's disappearing footprints.

4.

April Fools, the eve of the big day. Katherine sent Ron to visit Toony's Hardware in the old part of town. Ben Toony, grandson of a blacksmith and great-grandson of a slave blacksmith, lived with his wife Martha and son, Isaac, in a spacious flat above their store. The third floor, one-bedroom apartment with river views in the winter and leafy maples the remainder of the year sat vacant.

Ron had met Isaac the previous summer while working side-by-side during the steel mill's one-month maintenance period, shoveling ash eight hours a day. And, like members of a chain gang, dirt and sweat formed a bond between the two boys.

Ron stood on the second-story landing, finger hovering over the buzzer. This ain't right, he thought. When the doorbell sounded, he almost ran away. But Martha Toony answered, the scent of cooking and warmth wafted through the screen.

"May I help you," she asked, loosening her apron.

"Sorry to bother you, Mrs. Toony. Is Isaac around?"

"May I ask who's calling?"

"Oh, yeah. I'm Ron Kelly. Me and Isaac are friends from work."

"Isaac," she called, her voice as gentle as her kind brown eyes. "There's someone here to see you."

"I'll be right there, Mom," Isaac replied, his voice coming from somewhere in the back of the apartment.

"Won't you come in," Martha offered, holding the door open.

"No, thanks. I gotta speak with him in private, if that's okay?"

"Well, I understand. Can I offer you ice tea or something?"

"No, thanks, ma'am. I'm fine."

Isaac jogged to the door, fresh from the shower, dressed for a Friday night on the town. His mother rolled her eyes and left the boys alone.

Isaac smoothed pomade over his Little Richard-inspired pompadour. "Ron, what the hell you doin' in this part of town," he asked.

"Let's go to the street," Ron begged. "I've got some things to ask and I don't want anybody else to hear. It's important."

"Yeah, well, alright. What's the big mystery," Isaac inquired. Before Ron could answer, he yelled down the hall. "Mom. I'll be right back."

"Okay, son. But don't be long. Dinner's on."

The young men descended two flights of creaky stairs and stood under a streetlamp. Ron offered Isaac a smoke and they lit up.

"Lay it on me, man. What's goin' on?"

"I'm getting married."

"No? You?"

"Yeah, me."

"Who's the girl? When?"

"Someone you don't know but you know her old man and it's tomorrow."

"Tomorrow?" Isaac grabbed Ron's arm. "Wait, man. You gotta be kiddin' me. This is April Fools or something, ain't it?"

Ron noticed Mrs. Toony looking out the front window. He cupped Isaac's elbow and steered him from the light and into shadows that blanketed the sidewalk.

"This is no joke," Ron said.

"What can I do?" Isaac started to laugh. "What do you need from me, an instruction booklet? A waiter?"

"Very funny, Isaac. I need a friend. Katherine and me need a friend. That's her name, Katherine O'Hara."

"You mean O'Hara... company cop O'Hara?"

"That's him. And the guy hates everything about me."

They walked down the street and decided to sit on brick steps, the only identifiable thing remaining of the Davis and Son Grocery.

"What the hell happened to this place," Ron asked.

"I dunno exactly. It was some kind of electrical fire. But I don't give a shit about that now. Tell me why O'Hara hates you? What'd you do to him?"

"I'm Protestant and he's Catholic."

Isaac shook his head in disbelief. "You're talkin 'bout religion? That's it? Shit, man. At least you're the same color." He took hold of Ron's shoulders. "If this guy O'Hara really hates you, you're about to have a ton of crap rain on your head."

"Katherine wants to get married just as much I do. She practically asked me," Ron said, searching his friend's eyes.

"Now I got it all figured out," Isaac continued.

"What figured out?"

"I thought those white guys at work avoided you because of me. Like you got some disease that'd melt 'em faster than the blast furnace if they got too close. But now I know what it is."

"What the hell you talking about?"

"You're fuckin' nuts. That's what you are. You could have any of the white girls, probably a few of the soul sisters, too. But what do you do? You choose to live in a tub of shit."

"I don't need a sermon, Isaac. My people turned against me. Katherine's family says I'm robbing her soul."

"Well, who the hell am I," Isaac asked. "The Lord Jesus? What can I do?"

"Justice of the Peace McCarthy is marrying us and nobody from our families would ever consent to stand at the wedding. Will you be my best man?"

"You're a piece of work, man," Isaac said, scratching stubble on his chin. "Yeah. I guess if you're jumpin' off the bridge I'll tag along for the ride."

"Oh. I forgot one thing," Ron said. "We need a place to stay and none of the vacant apartments in our part of town are available, if you know what I mean. I remember you mentioned your dad had a spare place. Would he rent it to us?"

Isaac jingled change in his pocket. "There's only one way to find out," he said, turning toward home

Ron jumped up and grabbed his arm. " What's your old man gonna think about me and Katherine?"

Isaac grinned. "A man like my Dad," he said, "my people? Hell. If we don't understand hate no one will."

Isaac broke free. "C'mon. "Let's get going. I don't know about you, but I gotta get up early. I'm best man at a wedding tomorrow."

As they jogged, a thought came to Isaac. "Hey, why tomorrow? Did you knock her up or something?"

"No, Isaac. I didn't knock her up. But she's made up her mind, and she said if we didn't get married now, we never would. She's got it all figured out. We've been waitin' for my old man and her father to pull the Saturday shift. They'll be stuck at the mill all day. That way we'll avoid any fireworks."

"She sounds like a smart chick. Let's go see my Dad."

5.

After leaving Toony's, Ron went to Gerber's. He arrived to find Katherine sitting at the soda fountain, finishing a burger and sipping a Nehi Wild Red. He plopped onto the stool next to hers and spun, howling like a rodeo rider.

"Baby, it's all set. We got a place to live and a best man. Did you have any luck?"

Katherine said nothing, chewing the last bits of burger.

"Did you have any luck, honey?" Ron said.

"No," she said. "I had zero luck. Not one of my girlfriends is willing to stand beside me."

She sat on her stool and wondered out loud, "What are we gonna do? We need another witness or the ceremony won't be legal."

"Maybe we should wait till you find somebody."

"No!" Her loud response caught him by surprise. "It's got to be tomorrow."

Ron stared toward the street as cars zoomed past the drugstore's front window.

"Leave it to me," Katherine said. "I'll find somebody. You just be sure to be at my house right after the eight a.m. whistle."

"I'll be there," Ron replied. "Isaac is meeting me at my house. Then we'll all catch the bus to Justice McCarthy's."

He took her by the arm and slid two dollars onto the counter. "C'mon, baby. I'll walk you home."

The couple filtered through bedlam that drifted on the main drag. Neon lights hung from dance halls, bars, massage parlors and peep shows offering compensation for forty hours slaving in the mill. If you had money, the welcome mat was out.

Among the row houses stuffed into the first block of Wood Street was Ron's. Gray light flickered through the first floor windows.

"My old man must be watching TV."

Katherine trembled. They walked and she began to wobble.

"Honey, you okay," he asked.

"Just a little tired. My stomach's churning. Must be nerves or the burger."

I'm gonna puke, rippled through her. She dashed behind a bush and out it came – soda, bread and meat. He wiped her face with his handkerchief.

"What's wrong?"

"I'll be fine. Just get me home."

When they reached the middle of the block, a green 1950 DeSoto packed with eight partying black teenagers wheeled to the curb. The radio blared Jackie Wilson. Isaac, wild eyed, poked his head out the driver's window. "Tomorrow." he yelled. The rear tires screeched and the car disappeared into the night.

"There goes my best man."

"Were there any girls in that car? Maybe one could stand for me?"

"Nah. I doubt it. Those guys are trollin' for trouble. I hope Isaac doesn't find any."

When Ron and Katherine hit the next block, they saw every light in the O'Hara house beaming, Mr. O'Hara pacing the front porch. They hid behind a parked truck.

"What time is it?" Her voice cracked.

"Ten-thirty."

"I told him ten. That I'd be back by ten"

"So? What's the big deal? You're thirty minutes late."

"Ron, you don't know my Dad."

"After tomorrow, it won't matter."

"Maybe. But that's tomorrow. Let me walk home by myself. There's no need for a blow-up."

Katherine walked the final hundred yards. Ron, out of sight, kept a vigilant eye. He watched as O'Hara ran to the sidewalk in a rant. Katherine spoke to her father, but Ron was too far away to hear. O'Hara took her by the arm, almost dragging her through the front door. After the house went dark, Ron came from hiding, lit a cigarette and flipped the match into a sewer grate.

"Tomorrow," he said, "she's belongs to me tomorrow, you dumb-ass cop."

He sprinted home, tiptoed past his dead-drunk father snoring on the couch, and slipped into bed, but barely slept.

6.

The sun cut into Isaac's sleep followed by a bang on the door. "Wake up! You told that boy you'd be at his house in thirty minutes. Get it in gear."

He untangled his eyelids. His head pounding, he surrendered to his father's orders. "Ah shit," he mumbled. "What time did I get in?"

Still clad in Friday-night duds, he stumbled to the bathroom, pissed a river, sucked water from the faucet like it was a nipple, and took a shower in record time. His only suit was laid out on the bed when he emerged clean but foggy-headed. His shoes were shined and a shirt and tie hung from a dresser knob. "What the…" he began, but his mother poked her head in the door.

"Hurry now. Your father and I will run you and your friends to Justice McCarthy's. You'll never make the bus."

Isaac half-ran and half-fell down two flights of stairs and into the back of the DeSoto, his father eyeballing him every step of the way.

"You're the worst-looking best man I've ever seen," he said.

Daylight gouged Isaac's eyes.

"Son," Mr. Toony said. "I know you're half drunk but listen to me. You're gettin' in the middle of something. You know that, don't you?" He backed out of the driveway, Isaac slouched in the rear seat; his head slumped in his palms.

"Boy! You listening?"

"Yeah, I hear you, Pop. You don't have to yell."

"This wedding, you're puttin' yourself between warring parties. You have to remember who we are."

The car rolled down the street, past the charred building. Ben tapped on the window.

"See that, Isaac? That's what happens when you get in the middle."

Isaac struggled to focus.

"See what? That lump of charcoal and brick that's been there forever? What's it got to do with my headache?"

His father's eyes sharpen as the car passed through the center of town.

"I know the story you've been told, but it wasn't an electrical problem that destroyed that building. That's what our people had to believe. We didn't want anymore trouble." Ben took a deep breath. "It was bottles of gasoline that burnt the Davis store. It went up like dried hay. Tom and his wife got out but their boy didn't."

"Pop. That's ancient history. What's it got to do with today?"

Ben concentrated on driving until the car slowed to a halt in front of the Kelly house. Ron was on the porch, valise in hand, and mother at his side.

Ben turned to the back seat. "The person who tossed those bombs was Bob Kelly. Your friend's father."

Isaac's mouth flew open. "What?"

"Son, to you it might be ancient history, but for us it's as real as real gets.

"Why didn't he go to jail?"

"Back then white boys didn't serve time for hurting our people. But your mother and me, we talked it over. It's time to stop letting wrong have its way. We know we're taking a chance, but your friend, Ron, doesn't seem to be a bit like his father."

Ron trotted to the car. "Mr. and Mrs. Toony, what are

you doing here?"

Ben rolled down the window. "We decided to give your party a lift," he said. "I hope you don't mind."

"No, sir. Not a bit."

Ron put his suitcase in the trunk, hopped in the backseat, and rolled down the window. "I'll talk to you later," he called to his mother.

"Doesn't she want to join us," Martha asked.

"No, ma'am. It'd be better to keep her in the dark. That way, when my father wonders where I am, she won't have to lie."

* * *

After puttering a distance, the car stopped in front of the last house on the left. Katherine and her mother stood on the curb. Katherine's beige dress clung to her. Ron jumped out, took her valise and placed it in the trunk.

"You're beautiful," he said.

"What's this," she asked, looking toward the car full of Toonys. "I thought we were taking the bus."

"Honey, I'd like you to meet our new landlords, Martha and Ben. They've offered to drive us." Ron's eyes shifted to Mrs. O Hara's. His body stiffened "Good morning, ma'am."

Anticipating friction, Ben hopped out of the front seat. "Good morning, Mrs. O'Hara, I'm Ben Toony." He gestured to the front of the car. "This is my wife, Martha and the sleepy-eyed soul in the back is my son, Isaac."

"Pleased to meet you," she said. Her plump features lightened with her earnest smile.

Ben glanced at his watch. "We'd better get a move on. It's –" The steel mill's 8:00 a.m. whistle blasted. "One thing you always know in this town," he shouted. "When it's eight a.m., noon or four." The whistle drone died. Ben continued, "And don't worry, Mrs. O'Hara. We'll take good care of your daughter."

"Mother's coming with us," Katherine said. "She's my witness."

"Your witness?" Ron asked.

"Ronald," Mrs. O'Hara said. "Don't look so surprised. I'm not opposed to young people finding happiness. I'm sure your mother feels the same."

"Feels? She's scared to death to feel anything about this."

"Well, Mr. O'Hara will not be pleased when he comes home to find that his daughter has run off and married." Mrs. O' Hara looked toward the mill. "But I know him," she continued. "There's not a mean bone in him and he'll get used to the idea. It'll take a while, but he'll come around."

Ben flung open the rear door. "Isaac, wake up," he commanded. "Get your wine-soaked head out of the clouds and butt in the front with mother and me. The bride and groom deserve the honor of riding with Mrs. O'Hara."

* * *

Over at the mill, a line of grumbling workers slinked toward the guardhouse. Bob Kelly stood at its tail, rattling obscenities, his security badge in hand and lunch pail under his arm.

O'Hara methodically checked each employees ID.

"Ah, Jesus Christ," Kelly shouted. "No wonder it's taking so damn long."

The 8:00 a.m. whistle blasted.

"Fucking great," he continued. "Now the bastard has me punchin' in late on Saturday. What're ya doin', O'Hara? Checkin' assholes?" He moved to the guardhouse.

"Let's see the badge," O'Hara said. He grabbed it from

Kelly's hand and slapped it on the counter. "And now, the lunch pail, if you please?"

"What do ya want with my lunch?"

O'Hara stood with outstretched hand. "If you want to work today, let me take a look in that lunchbox."

"Piss on ya," Kelly said as he handed it over.

O'Hara flipped the lid, his eyes reflecting pure satisfaction: a pint of whiskey.

"Well, just as I heard. You've been getting a snoot-full while runnin' the crane on the dock. Holy Mary, man! You'll take someone's head off operatin' that thing shit-faced. But since I'm a forgivin' man," he said. "I'll hold this and not report you."

"So, now ya stealin' whiskey?"

"Kelly, I'm warnin' you."

"Oh, fuck ya, and ya scumbag family."

O'Hara glowered, his fist clenched, his jaw clamped.

Kelley laughed. "What? All pissed-off, are ya? Ya gonna go for your pea shooter, ya coward," he said. "Everyone knows there's not an ounce of lead in it."

O'Hara stood stiff.

Kelly sensed an opportunity. "Yeah, ya think I don't know the story."

O'Hara's arms went limp.

Kelly raised his voice for all to hear. "Too bad the guy ya lent ya gun to didn't tell his four-year-old it was loaded before he sneaked up behind his Daddy and said, 'Stick 'em up,' and pulled the trigger. That little kid splashed his old man's brains all over the kitchen. Absolute genius, O'Hara."

All O'Hara could do was take it.

Kelly belly-laughed, collected his ID badge, his lunch pail, and joined waiting friends on the other side of the checkpoint.

"Oh, it's the killer, O'Hara. I'm frightened outta me shorts," he yelled. "And ya can keep the whiskey. There's plenty more."

O'Hara stood alone in the hut, watching Kelly and his gang head toward the dock. And for the first time in many years, he pulled a bullet from his cartridge belt.

7.

Halfway to Justice McCarthy's, Ben stopped at a gas station. "We there," Isaac asked, stirred from his hangover.

"No, son. The justice doesn't open until nine and we need fuel. If you ladies would like to freshen up, this'd be the time."

A glassy-eyed attendant leered at the O'Hara women as they walked to the restroom. "Nice legs," he said and turned to Ben. "What can I get ya?"

"Fill 'er."

"Sure thing, boy."

Ben remained with the car, watching the attendant wipe soot from the windshield and pump gas. When the wedding party returned, the attendant winked at Katherine. She took her mother by the arm and slid into the back seat.

"That'll be five bucks, boy."

Ben handed him four singles and loose change.

"Boy," the attendant said, counting the money. "I bet you're chauffeuring these fine white women to a camp meetin' or funeral, aren't ya?"

"You could say that."

"What's that mean? Are ya some kinda smart-ass?"

"I'm sorry." Ben started the engine. "I meant to say that we're on our way to praise hope and the death of ignorance. You fool."

"Ya black son of a bitch." The attendant lurched, but Ben stepped on the gas.

"Benjamin, you shouldn't incite people like that," Martha said, holding on to the armrest.

"I know, I know. But when that guy called me 'boy' it

got my butt cooking."

"You'd better not let it get too hot or you'll be ham."

"I know. I'm sorry."

Mrs. O'Hara touched Ben's shoulder. "I apologize for what that man said."

"Who, that ignorant fool? He couldn't lick your boots if he stood on the highest ladder."

"People like that make me ashamed," Ron said.

Ben chuckled. "You think you folks cornered the market on idiots? We got plenty."

* * *

As the car sped away from the filling station, everyone laughed except Katherine. She stared at Ron's hand intertwined with hers. Her stomach churned in anticipation of the first act of her grand charade.

* * *

Justice McCarthy answered the door with a long, "May I help you?"

"Good morning, sir," Ben said. "I have two young people who want to get married."

"It's a glorious morning. Come on in."

His dark wood office was an unkempt sea of books and magazines. The oak desk with piles of newspapers served as centerpiece. "Don't mind the mess," McCarthy said. "I'm sorting through a few things."

Katherine and the wedding party navigated the clutter. Down the hall, the chapel stood in stark contrast to the office – pristine white walls and plush red carpet. There were three rows of church pews on either side of the aisle and a small lectern at its end. In the corner sat a small pump organ.

"Oh, you have music for the service," Martha said.

"Used to," McCarthy mumbled. "My wife played, but she died."

"Oh, I'm sorry."

"Don't be. We had fifty good years."

* * *

McCarthy's words rang in Katherine's ears. I'll be lucky if I make it fifty days, she thought.

* * *

McCarthy moved to the lectern, almost preacher-like in his black waistcoat and clip-on bow tie. "During the war," he said, "I'd have couples eloping with no witnesses. We bent the rules back then. Most of 'em were all alone and scared to death." His arms were so long they seemed to touch everyone. "But it looks like we have a complete wedding party today. Who's the best man?" Isaac's hand poked the air. "And the maid of honor?" Mrs. O'Hara stepped forward. Seeing her wedding band, McCarthy said, "Excuse me, matron of honor. Is the father of the bride coming?"

"No, he isn't available. He's a policeman at the mill."

"Ah. Pulled the Saturday shift, did he? Tough break. Well," he continued, glancing at Ben, "looks like you're giving the bride away."

"It would be an honor, sir."

McCarthy turned to Martha. "Ma'am, you can sit in the front, if you like."

"I play the organ," Martha said. And I remember the wedding march."

"That's a fine suggestion. Please make yourself comfortable."

He looked to Katherine. "And you must be the nervous young bride."

"Yes," she whispered, "I'm Katherine O'Hara."

McCarthy took Isaac and Ron by the shoulders like two chess pieces and moved them to the left of the lectern. "You boys stand here." He looked to Ben. "Sir, you, the bride and Mrs. O'Hara go to the vestibule. When you hear the wedding march, Mrs. O'Hara will walk down the aisle and stand to the right. You and Katherine will follow. She will stand next to her mother and you'll stand behind the bride." He motioned to Martha. "That's when the music stops and I start."

McCarthy flipped his wrist. Martha pumped the foot bellows and fingered the keys. The old organ came to life and its pipes squeezed out the wedding theme. For Katherine the music sounded more like a requiem. She started down the aisle. It might as well have been the death march. For the sake of her parents' lives, she moved forward, each step bringing her closer to a spiritual abyss. She stared at Ron. His eyes, shaped like his father's, focused on her. His mouth, similar to the mouth that grunted and groaned like an animal while sucking her breasts, formed a smile. Her mother stood helpless, tears dripping. Katherine took a deep breath and summoned all her strength, committed to what she must do. At Ron's side, her mother whispered in her ear, "Are you sure about this?"

Katherine looked her in the eye and squeezed her hand. "Yes."

All went as planned until McCarthy asked for the rings. Katherine saw Ron's face turn white as he ran his hands over his suit coat and through his trouser pockets. "I, I left them at home on my dresser."

"Do you want to proceed without the rings?" McCarthy asked.

Dear God, Katherine silently prayed. Don't call it off. I

can't go through this again.

"Wait." Mrs. O'Hara removed her wedding band and handed it to Ron. It was the first time it had left her finger since placed there twenty-five years earlier. Ben slipped his wedding band from his finger and presented it to Katherine.

McCarthy continued the ceremony. Ron slipped Mrs. O'Hara's band on her daughter's finger. Katherine winced, sliding Ben's ring over Ron's finger.

McCarthy took Ron's hand and placed it over Katherine's. "Is there anyone who says these people should not be joined in holy matrimony? If so, please step forward or forever hold your peace." Katherine silently screamed, *me.*

With no takers, McCarthy declared, "And what has been joined by God let no man put asunder. By the power invested in me, I now pronounce you man and wife. You may kiss the bride."

Ron's lips tasted like poison. His embrace chilled her, for she knew that later that night he would be between her legs. But to complete the final act of her sacrifice she would have to permit his advances.

After the service, Isaac ran ahead of the others. He stood in the parking lot with the car door open. "This way to the honeymoon suite," he said.

* * *

The car motored along stretches of highway scarred by years of trucks caravanning iron and steel. A few miles later, a sign denoted the city limits.

WELCOME TO BATTLE HYMN
STEEL TOWN U.S.A.

"We headed home?" Isaac said.

"My original plan was Gerber's for a late breakfast," Ron said.

Katherine exhibited the first sign of enthusiasm. "I'm starved."

"You feeling better, sweetheart," her mother said. "You weren't well this morning."

"I'm fine. It was nerves."

Martha spoke over her shoulder. "You're all coming to our place for a sit-down meal. And you will join us, won't you Mrs. O'Hara?"

"It's a wonderful offer, but no thank you. I have things at home that need my attention. I'm afraid this will be a hard day and a very long night."

The car stopped at the Kelly's. Katherine slid closer to her mother. "I'll get the rings and be back in a flash." Ron jogged to the house. Katherine's feet tapped the floorboards. A minute later, with the wedding rings in hand, Ron hopped into the car.

Down the street, Ben parked in front of the O'Hara's. "Mrs. O'Hara," he said, "Let me help you."

"There's no need, Mr. Toony. I can make it on my own."

Katherine clutched her mother's arm. "Mother," she said. "Maybe I should wait for Daddy to come home?"

"No. Your place is with your husband." Mrs. O'Hara turned to Ron. "Take care of her. She's all we have." She kissed Katherine goodbye, and as the old car pulled away, she read the words finger-etched on its soot-covered trunk.

"Ron and Katherine Just Married."

8.

The 4:00 o'clock whistle filled the air. Forty minutes later, right on schedule, O'Hara strolled through the front door and hung his holster. "Katherine? Elizabeth? I'm home."

"In here, John, in the kitchen."

"Smells good," his happy voice reverberated down the hallway. "What's on the stove?"

"Pigs in a blanket."

"Only two places," he said, entering the kitchen. "Where is she?"

"Out."

"With that Kelly boy?"

"How were things at the mill?"

He grunted and sat. "Nothing more than the usual Saturday. Guys sneakin' booze in lunch boxes."

"You hungry, sweetheart?"

"Elizabeth, you're doing lots of talkin' but not much tellin'." He got up and snatched a can of beer from the refrigerator. "Where's our girl?"

"She's with Ron. And you know, you should give that boy half a chance."

"I might as well invite his father for dinner." He took a swig.

"Do you know Ron," Mrs. O'Hara asked. "Have you ever taken a moment to consider that he might be a decent person and nothing like his father?"

He rested his forehead on the back of his hand, sipping beer. "How could anyone live under that roof and not be influenced by that SOB?"

"Well, for one thing," she said, "Ronald doesn't drink. Katherine told me so this morning."

"So what does that mean," Mr. O'Hara mocked. "It just makes it easier to hide who he really is."

"You don't mean that." She spooned two cabbage rolls onto a plate. "I know who he is," she continued. "I've spent time with him, and a good part of it was today."

"Oh, Lord. Help us. Now you condone the thing? What about faith? Her salvation?"

She sat across the table. "You know that we have an Irish Catholic in the White House, don't you?"

"What's that got to do with anything?"

"You don't see him and his wife running around 'the Protestants this, the Jews that.' They seem to know that God takes many forms. I think this is how young people feel nowadays. There's a unity of the spirit."

"Woman, what the hell are you talking about?"

She got up, reduced the heat on the simmering dinner, turned and spoke softly. "Our girl was married today."

"Married? Where? When? How?" He stood, his arms flailing, "She snuck out, did she? Did it behind our backs?"

Mrs. O'Hara gripped his arm. "Not behind our backs, John. Behind yours and Bob Kelly's. I was with them at Justice McCarthy's this morning."

Mr. O'Hara dropped into his seat. She knelt beside him.

"John, she's not dead. It's not the end of the world. There's no need to be upset."

"Upset? You and Katherine liken me to Bob Kelly. You couldn't talk to me?"

"I didn't want to condone her actions," she said. "Not like this, but I had to do something." She pulled him close. "I think our baby's pregnant."

* * *

Bob Kelly leaned on the bar, six shots of whiskey, three beers and a plate of hot dogs with baked beans in his gut. Paul Duffy, a fellow dockworker, stood next to him, eyebrows raised.

"I see you're takin' advantage of the free food tonight," Duffy teased.

"Aw, fuck off. Give us another shot here, Tommy," Kelly said.

"Savin' your money because you hired the Black chauffeur?"

"What the fuck ya talking about? Chauffeur?"

"Yeah, Kelly. Chauffeur."

Duffy grinned as he gave the bar the once-over, making sure his audience was tuned in. "Since I had the day off, I decided to come by our beloved pub for some liquid lunch," he began. "And wouldn't you know it. There I am, on the corner, waitin' for the light to change and this boogie-mobile comes rollin' to a stop."

Kelly turned and let loose with a ripe belch, but Duffy didn't miss a beat. His voice grew mysterious.

"I take a peek in the back seat and there he is. Your son's wearin' Sunday school clothes all cuddled up to O'Hara's' daughter."

"My boy with spooks and that Catholic? Ya havin' a go with me?"

"Me? No. Never. But wait. You haven't heard the best part." Duffy lifted his mug. "I'd like to offer a toast to the newlyweds."

The rest of the group cheered, "Here, here. Here, here."

"C'mon on. Won't you even toast your son's wedding?"

"Fuck off. Ya bastard."

"No. I'm dead serious. When the light changed, the car pulled away. Not too fast, mind you."

Once again, Duffy surveyed his audience. "Are you

ready for the punch-line."

"I knew ya was pullin' my leg."

"As the hunk of junk pulled away, I read the wedding announcement written on the trunk. *Ron and Katherine – Just Married.*"

Duffy crossed his heart and raised his right hand. "I swear to God. Looks like you got yourself a daughter today, and a Catholic one at that."

The bar erupted in laughter. Kelly threw his head back, poured a seventh shot down his gullet, and stomped out the door.

* * *

Mrs. Kelly was asleep on the couch when her husband burst into the house.

"Where the fuck is he? The bastard."

"What's wrong? What are you talking about?"

"Ya know damn well what I'm talking about, ya bitch. I told you to talk some sense into him."

He took a fist full of hair and smacked her face with the back of his hand. Blood dripped from both of her nostrils.

"Where the fuck is he?"

"No. No. Bob, you're drunk. Please, don't hit me." She covered her eyes. "I don't know what you're talking about."

"Don't give me that shit. I gave ya a chance." He delivered a square shot to her jaw, sending her to the couch. "That little fucker thinks he can do as he pleases, going against his own people, embarrassing his father."

Mrs. Kelly was out cold. Mr. Kelly returned to the bar.

* * *

"If you and Ronald care to, you can come to church services with us tomorrow," Martha offered, stacking the last of the dishes. Ron and Katherine looked at one another. "Not tomorrow, but some other Sunday would be great," Katherine said.

"I understand." Martha collected empty coffee cups. "Did you find the bedding and linens?"

"Yes. They're wonderful. Thank you." Katherine wrung her hands. "I didn't even think of setting up the apartment."

"You've had a lot on your mind and this is your wedding night. Ben and me wanted to give the two of you a little head start."

"Thanks, that's very nice," Ron said as he twiddled Katherine's hair. "Good night."

Katherine walked the one flight to the apartment, Ron hot on her tail. They paused in the doorway, his eyes fixed on hers. She toyed with his zipper. He swept her in his arms, carrying her like a trophy. Inside, he stripped her naked and lifted her to lip level, her legs clamped around his waist.

After several minutes, Katherine pulled him from bed and led him to the tiny couch. "Sit," she said and pushed him. "Tell me what you want?" Her strands of hair danced on his tongue.

"Straddle me," he said.

Katherine turned her head to the side, concealing tearing eyes.

Dear God, this is the only way. Please forgive me.

She wiped her eyes and nibbled his finger. "That's what I thought you'd say."

Ron noticed the moisture on her cheeks. "You're crying. What's wrong?"

"I can't believe this is really happening."

"Either can I."

"How's it feel?" she said. "Is this what you thought a good little Catholic girl could give you?"

His moans grew, and a streak of vengeance rushed through her. "I love you," he whispered. She pulled his head to her breasts. *That's your problem.*

* * *

Ron tiptoed to the window, opened it and took a deep breath. Sounds of the approaching warm weather wandered in – chirping tree frogs and clicking crickets. He returned to bed and lit a cigarette while Katherine slept.

As he reflected on the day, he heard a truck approach. After its engine shutdown there was a ping followed by breaking glass. The streetlight went dark. BB gun, he thought, familiar with the sound, for he had extinguished a few street lamps in his day.

Muffled voices drew him from his bride and back to the window. He crushed the Lucky on the windowsill and stood to the side, peering through the curtain. There were three men smoking cigarettes. One of them aimed a flashlight at the DeSoto's trunk.

From the apartment below came the rustling of furniture. The lamp in the Toony's living room seeped light to the sidewalk followed by footsteps trotting down the stairs. The cigarettes were dashed and the three figures retreated to the shadows. Ron looked on as Ben stood next to the DeSoto, rifle in hand. An engine backfired and roared off, fading until only crickets and frogs broke the silence. Ron slipped back into bed, but it would be hours before he slept.

9.

Mourning doves perched on the ledge, and their soulful whistle summoned Ron from his sleep. I'm the king of Battle Hymn, he thought, tapping on the bathroom door.

"Sweetie, do you want coffee," he asked.

"Wait, I can't hear you," she replied. "The shower's too loud."

She cut the water. Ron stuck his head in the door.

"Do you want coffee?"

Katherine poked her hand through the shower curtain. "My ears are plugged. Hand me a towel." He took hold of her arm and nudged her from the bath.

"Hey, not now." Dripping and naked, she pushed him away as he attempted to wrap her in a towel.

"Let me dry you," he whispered, pulling her close.

"I said not now. I just got clean."

"Good. I can dirty you up again."

"You don't understand, do you?"

Ron rubbed her backside.

"Seriously." She slapped his hand away. "I'm hungry," she said.

"Me, too."

"I don't think we're talking about the same thing. Get out of here."

She shooed him from the bathroom, but he jammed his foot in the door.

"What's wrong," he asked.

"Listen, Ron. A wedding isn't a free pass."

"What the hell?"

"I'll say when, where, how we do it." She dislodged his

foot and locked the door. "Now, what time is it?"

Ron chuckled and glanced at his watch. "Nine-thirty."

"Martha left some groceries. I'll make breakfast when I'm done in here."

"Okay," he replied, laughing off her rebuff. He opened his suitcase and took inventory of clothes, personal items and other things his mother had packed.

Katherine, wrapped from shoulder to knee in a towel, emerged from the bathroom.

"You look like a terrycloth flower," he said.

"Give me a half-hour without food and you'll see me turn into a weed." She tucked her hair in another towel and piled it on her head.

"Why don't you get breakfast started," he said. "I gotta run home."

"Home? This is your home. What do you need?"

"My work boots. I can't show up in dress shoes."

"Why not?" She teased, "You'll look like one of those executive-types."

He felt the urge to strip her. His hand slid under the towel and pinched a nipple.

She broke free. "I said, I'll tell you when and where."

She turned and stared out at the river with its dead branches and everything from old refrigerators to broken furniture flowing downstream.

"I'm just goofin' around," he said. "But about the boots, it's serious. I could get my toes cut off while workin' the dock. I need steel tips for protection."

Get away from me, she thought when his chin explored the crook of her neck.

"Listen, baby," he said. "I'll shoot over to my mom's and be back before the bacon's crisp."

* * *

Ron cut through backyards, following paths known only to the children of Battle Hymn. As he neared his street he thought of any other items that he might need, but there were none.

He leapt to the porch with a thud and took a deep breath. There were no scents of bacon or cigars—unusual for a Sunday—but the door opened with its familiar creak. On the couch, his father dressed in yesterday's work clothes, grunted and snorted a facsimile of sleep. In the kitchen, beef stew congealed on the stovetop, two undisturbed place settings on the table. A turning quart of milk sat on the Lazy Susan. Upstairs, he collected his work boots, went to the master bedroom, and touched his mother's shoulder.

"Ma, you awake?"

She shuddered, hands covering her face. "Is that you, Ron?"

"Yeah, it's me."

"I thought it was him."

"What're you talking about, Ma?"

He moved her hands and bit his knuckle. "The bastard! I'll kill him!"

"No. It's my fault. I asked for it."

"Ma, don't lie. That excuse worked years ago, when I was too young to know better."

"Oh please, Ronnie. Don't do anything."

Ron smacked his palm against the old headboard.

"You're right," he said. "Let's get your robe."

They went next door to Mrs. Magee's, their aged, nosey neighbor. After a single knock, Mrs. Magee answered as if she had been expecting them. "Yes? Oh! At it again, is he?"

"Please see to her, will you, Mrs. Magee?"

"Well, all right. Come in, Margaret."

Ron returned to his living room, slipped out of his

penny-loafers, laced up the steel-tip boots, and stood next to the couch, nudging his father's beer gut.

"Wake up, you bastard. Wake the fuck up."

Mr. Kelly rolled.

"Oh, ya little shit," he mumbled. "I've been waitin' for ya."

He jumped to his feet, his haymaker clipping Ron's chin. He tried the other fist but Ron ducked and shot a right hand to his neck, steering him to the wall.

I could kill you in a second, Ron thought.

"If you touch her," he said, jamming his fist to his father's crotch, "if you so much as look at my mother, I'll hunt you down. Do you hear me?"

A steamy mess flooded Kelly's pants. After relinquishing the death grip, Ron demanded, "Do you hear me, you bastard?"

Mr. Kelly, breathless, nodded. Ron raised a fist. His father flinched. Message delivered, Ron shoved him to the couch.

* * *

Mrs. Magee sat on the sofa, about to lecture Mrs. Kelly on the ill effects of disobeying her husband. Ron tapped on the front door and entered. He knelt and held his mother's hand.

"Ma," he said, "Come to my place."

He lifted her chin. Purple framed her eye, the corner of her mouth a sagging lump of flesh.

"No, Ron, my place is here." Her words struggled to clear swollen lips. "I'm his wife. It's my duty," she sobbed.

"He'll do it again, Ma."

"Ron, he only wanted to know where you were."

"The only thing I know," Ron said, "is that he'll do it again."

She touched his chin. "Ronnie, I heard every word you said to him. After what you did he won't be bothering me anymore."

"Should we call for the doctor," Mrs. Magee asked.

"No, I'll be fine."

"How about the cops," Ron asked.

"What? And bring them and their snooping ways into our lives? That'll give us a whole new set of troubles," Mrs. Kelly warned.

Ron stood. She looked at him like a vanquishing hero. "I'll stay here for a few hours, son. Your father will come to his senses. It'll be all right. You go tend to your life."

"But what if he tries it again? Are you sure?"

"Yes, son. You go. I've been through this before. I'll be okay."

He asked Mrs. Magee, "Got a pencil and paper?"

"Sure, boy."

"Here," he said, jotting a number. "Take this, Ma. If there's a hint of trouble, you call. Tell 'em who you are. They'll get word to me lightning quick." He turned to Mrs. Magee. "How 'bout you taking the number and call if you hear anything?"

"Sure I will. I always keep my ears opened."

He touched his mother's forehead, hoping to sponge away the pain. "I love you, Ma."

"I know you do, son. And I love you."

"Are you sure you'll be okay?"

"You go. I'll have a visit with Mrs. Magee." Ron stood in the open doorway. "I'm proud of you," she said. He left her with a smile.

* * *

The shadow of violence followed Ron. Struck by a bolt of childhood memory, he saw the image of his mother lying on the kitchen floor, his father over top of her, hands wrapped around her neck. He could still hear her gasps and see her eyes plead for help. *Leave my Mommy alone! Leave my Mommy alone!* His voice had gone unheard as his father strangled her. He felt the Roy Rodgers toy pistol snug in his little hand as it slammed against his father's head. *Leave my Mommy alone!* Another swipe had caught his father's attention, snapped him out of his drunken rage, and sent him stumbling out the door.

Ron's eyes welled as he recalled cuddling up in the fold of her breast, as she lay unconscious.

* * *

Isaac buffed the family car to a shine. Ron rounded the corner.

"Hey," Isaac yelled. "Take a look at this thing. Amazing what a bath will do, isn't it?"

Ron grunted, "Yeah."

"What do you mean? This car never looked better. It's a chick magnet."

"Yeah, whatever you say."

"Why the hell you so long in the face, my man? And why you carrying good shoes and wearin' shit-kickers on a Sunday?"

"I wanted to stretch them out."

Isaac wrung the rag. "They'll get plenty of stretch when we join that maintenance crew tomorrow," he said.

"I completely forgot about that," Ron said. "I don't have to work with my old man on the dock. I'm on the maintenance crew." He yipped like he had just won a reprieve from death row.

"Where's Katherine?"

"She's with Mom and Dad. She waited but you never showed so she had breakfast with us."

"Thanks, Isaac. You're a lifesaver." Ron ran up the wooden stairs, leaving Isaac to murmur, "Man. If that's what gettin' married does, count me out."

* * *

Ben rushed to answer the door. "Come into the living room and grab a seat, son. You don't want to miss this. Martin Luther King is appearing on a news program."

With Ben's eyes fixed on TV, Ron sat and thought, who the hell is Martin Luther King? After enough time passed to be polite he asked, "Is Katherine here?"

"She and Martha walked down to the river," Ben said. "Girls will be girls. They're off pickin' daffodils. Hey, by the way. Katherine mentioned that you went home this morning. What for?"

"Just to get my boots. That's all." Ron let loose with a big yawn. He stretched his arms and legs, staring at Ben, thinking of him standing with a rifle in his hand. Ben gave a small chuckle. "I guess you didn't get much sleep last night." He turned from the TV in time to catch a look of surprise on Ron's face.

"No, no, son," he said. "Don't get me wrong. I'm not being rude or anything. I mean you must have a lot on your mind this morning. Married and all, living here with us in this part of town."

"I ran into my father."

"Now that's good cause for creases in a forehead. How's he feel about what you've done?"

"I think he's taking it out on my mother."

"Oh, in what way?"

Ron avoided eye contact. "He's just giving her a tough time. That's all. He wants to know where Katherine and me are living. She can't tell him because she doesn't know, and that's the way I want it."

"What'd you say to him?" Ben sounded concerned.

"I –" Ron's brain locked then unfroze. "I told him to leave Ma alone and not to worry about me or Katherine."

Ron lit a cigarette. "Mr. Toony, did you hear the streetlamp get busted with a BB gun last night?"

Ben replied, "You heard that? It was just some pranksters." He flicked his hand as if shooing a fly. "They come around from time to time."

Ron dropped ash in the tray. "I saw three guys shine a light at your car," he said. "They took off when you showed up with a rifle."

Ben reached over and lowered the volume on the TV. "Ronald," he said, "I think there's a few things you need to know."

As Ron listened, Ben told of the Davis tragedy. When he heard that his father was suspected of setting the fire, but never arrested, he pounded the table.

"That bastard! How could my mother marry him?"

"Quiet, boy. Don't shout. You want the whole neighborhood to hear? Don't blame your mother," he whispered. "She probably didn't know who he was until she was good and married with you on the way. She got stuck."

Ron smashed his cigarette in the ashtray.

"Mr. Toony," he began.

Ben cut him off. "It's high time you called me Ben."

"Ben, you knew this stuff and still rented us the apartment?"

He rested his hand on Ron's knee. "Son," he said, "when you and Isaac came to me that night and told me about your situation, I knew you were nothing like your father. Nothing."

His attention returned to the broadcast. "Let's listen," he said. "Here's Dr. King."

At that moment, the women entered the room carrying bunches of flowers. Ron's eyes met Katherine's. Her smile wilted when she saw he wore work boots.

"What did you do, eat breakfast with your family?" she asked.

"No," Ron replied.

"Well, then what kept you? The bacon got more than crisp."

Ron stood, wiping his palms on his pants. "I had a talk with my old man."

Her flowers dropped to the floor. "What does he want? He's not coming here, is he?"

"No, Katherine. Don't get all worked up."

"I'm not ready to meet him, Ron." She bent to collect the flowers. Ron helped.

As they knelt, he noticed her hand trembling. "Don't worry, Katherine," he whispered. "He's not coming here."

Martha came from the kitchen. "You hungry, Ron? I have plenty left."

"Thanks," Katherine replied, brushing back her hair. "But I want to cook him his first breakfast as a married man."

"I understand," Martha said as she joined Ben on the couch.

Ron and Katherine held hands, hers as clammy as his. "Let's go upstairs," she suggested. "You can tell me more about what your father said."

10.

Easter Sunday, Saint Ann's was packed to the balcony. A long line of parishioners took communion and knelt in pews. Three mournful gongs signaled Father Ryan to return the Chalice to its tiny gold hut atop the altar. The organ played a calliope for the faithful, the discordant choir sang along. After he blessed his flock, the priest made a procession down the aisle, three fresh-faced altar boys in tow. At the front door, he greeted members of the congregation, among them the O'Haras.

"Elizabeth, as beautiful as ever." he said. "How are you?"

"I've been better."

His eyes met Mr. O'Hara's. "Katherine's still not with us, I see."

Mr. O'Hara stuttered, "I…we…"

"It's okay, John. I know you are in a difficult position."

He took hold of O'Hara's hand and joined it to his wife's in a one-for-all-and-all-for-one gesture. "A few weeks back, I heard her confession," he said. "I told her how the Church looks upon these matters and how her soul is at risk if she doesn't confess and chooses to side with Satan." His wafer-thin smile cut across his face. "You folks are in for a rough time. I'll ask extra prayers. Now go in peace."

Arm in arm, Mr. and Mrs. O'Hara walked down the steps and onto the sidewalk, sensing the gawks of fellow Catholics. Once in their house, he sat at the kitchen table, drumming a military cadence with his fingers. She donned an apron, preparing what should have been a joyous feast.

His palms flattened on the table. "Elizabeth? What did we do wrong?"

Her knuckle dug into a bowl of baking dough. "I don't know if we had any power to stop this," she said.

"How do you mean?"

"Times are different, not like when we were coming up." She stopped kneading and turned to him. "Today, young people seem to be on a different path. They do things and feel what ever they want. I don't know what it is, but they live their lives like there's no tomorrow." She thrust her hand into the unformed paste, twisting and churning. "Solid faith is the best thing we can offer her," she said. "Let's hope it takes hold."

Mr. O'Hara's splayed fingers raked his face. "The church has excommunicated her for marrying that Protestant. You know that, don't you?"

His wife, deeper into the conversation than intended, said, "If she's pregnant, at least she's married."

"Oh that's great. That's just wonderful. Hopefully, we won't be further disgraced by her stomach bulging too soon."

"I'm not positive she's having a baby, John. It's just a gut feeling. Besides, if we want her in our lives, if her children are to call us grandfather and grandmother, we'll have to find a way to accept what's happened." She pulled her hands from the turgid lump. "Ron's nothing like his father. I'm sure of it."

"Let me give it some time," he said, "and I'll pray for tolerance." He returned to drumming the table. "Why did they go to the old part of town? It's dangerous over there, don't they know?"

"That part of town never handed out an ounce of hurt,"

she replied. "It's only been on the receiving end. If understanding is what Katherine and Ronald need, that's where they'll find it." She came to the table. "John, you should visit her. Let her know we love her."

"I will. But I need time. Ronald Kelly's my son-in-law."

11.

On Monday, Isaac and Ron reported to the tin shed known as the maintenance office. The foreman, a lanky, pockmark-faced man, met them at the door.

"Here, take these," he said, shoving tools in Ron's face. "You'll need 'em." He looked past Ron to where Isaac stood, ten yards back. "Hey, you. Get your ass over here."

Isaac poked his own chest. "Me?"

"Yeah you, Midnight. Don't be a wise ass. Go fetch the water."

Ron carried a pick and two shovels. Isaac hauled a five-gallon water Thermos.

"Get in the back of the truck," the foreman yelled as he sat in the passenger seat. "We're late."

The boys hunkered in the payload, the truck bouncing its way to the first mess.

"Here you go, fellas." The driver hit the brakes, his jowls jiggling. "Twenty tons of coke that fell off a flat bed last night. Get your lazy butts into it and clear the roadway."

Isaac played Steppin' Fetchit. "Yaz sir. I'm a clearin' it."

"Smart-ass," the driver replied, spitting a wad of tobacco-infused mucus at Isaac's feet.

The boys dug at the ten-foot mound, clearing the roadway one scoop at a time. They took ten-minute breaks every hour then continued digging. When the noon whistle sounded, the truck returned to collect them for lunch back at the maintenance shed.

Upon seeing their progress, the foreman tsk-tsked, "You boys are takin' so damn long it looks like you like this job."

Ron and Isaac tossed their shovels on the heap and hopped in the back of the truck.

"Hell," the driver said, "you look like goddamn twins." The coke dust had coated the boys inside and out.

Back at the shed, they washed and ate sandwiches at a makeshift table. The foreman and a few other lifers were in a private office. After taking a phone call, that office filled with hooting and hollering. Thirty minutes later, the driver and the foreman emerged, backslapping and stinking of liquor.

"All right," the foreman said. "Let's get you asshole-buddies back at it. Get in the truck."

On the ride, Ron nudged Isaac. "I thought maintenance would be better than the dock."

"It doesn't matter where I work," Isaac said. "It all sucks."

"We've gotta find a way to get out of this piece-of-shit job."

"Let me know when you find it. I'll be right on your ass."

"As of this moment, I'm looking," Ron said and lit a Lucky. "Hell, I can't support a wife doing this. And what about kids?"

Isaac chuckled. "Big Daddy Ron. I can see you changin' smelly diapers."

Ron looked off to the rust-tinted landscape. "Yeah, Big Daddy. That's me."

The truck stuttered to a halt.

"All assholes and wannabes get out and start digging," the foreman yelled.

The boys hopped off the truck and started working the pile. They would be there until the 4:00 p.m. whistle.

* * *

On their second day as maintenance workers, Isaac and Ron arrived early, hoping to take some of the sting out of the foreman. Isaac loaded tools while Ron, in need of a bathroom, entered the shed. The foreman and the driver were in the office, door shut, voices hushed. Ron moved closer.

The driver spoke, "How long does Bob want us to fuck with these kids?"

"He didn't say," the foreman replied. "We'll keep pushin' Midnight until he explodes. When that happens, Bob's boy will try to save him. That's when the fun begins. O'Hara will have to arrest his nigger-lovin' son-in-law."

Ron clenched his jaw.

"Wait till they see the present waitin' for 'em," the driver chuckled.

"Yeah, it should be a good one," the foreman replied.

Ron crept from the shed, deciding to pee later. Isaac's head poked over the payload's wood panels. Ron scurried into the truck bed, securing the tailgate. "Isaac, we're in for it," he warned.

"Now what?"

"I heard the foreman and the driver talking about fucking with us. My father's working 'em like puppets. He's directing the operation."

"No disrespect, but what kind of fool do you have for a father?"

"I didn't choose him."

"Sorry, I didn't mean it to sound like your fault," Isaac said. "But what the hell can they do? Call us names? Get us pissed off so we do something to get canned?"

"My father's capable of much more."

Isaac cast his eyes toward the shed. "I know what he's capable of."

Ron grabbed Isaac's arm. "What do you mean?"

"Yeah, I know about your old man. My dad gave me the lowdown on what he did to the Davis family."

Ron's grip eased. "I just found out about it, too."

Isaac love-tapped his arm. "It was a long time ago. You didn't do it. Your father did."

The foreman and the driver came to the vehicle. Isaac and Ron popped up from the truck bed.

"Well, looky here," the foreman said. "If it ain't the Catholic-lovin' whoremaster and his lawn jockey."

Ron's hand balled to a fist. Isaac pinned it to the truck bed.

"Yaz sur, Mr. Foreman," he slurred. "That'd be us. The whoremaster and his lawn jockey."

"We know how to handle a smart-ass boy like you," the driver snarled, preparing to yank Isaac out of the vehicle.

The foreman intervened. "Let's get goin'," he said. "There's shit to shovel."

The driver drove with a new sense of purpose, hitting every available pothole. The boys braced their bodies and absorbed whatever the road presented.

When they arrived at the coke pile the driver slammed the brakes, sending tools and boys flying. Ron landed upside down, his back to the passenger compartment.

"That fuck," he cried out.

"No, Ron, that's what they want," Isaac said as he caught Ron's pant leg. "Take it from me. Don't fall for it."

The foreman grinned, "Hey, looks like the lumps of coke had babies that shit themselves last night."

As the boys hopped from the truck, it hit them. All the coke they shoveled yesterday had been put back in its original pile, topped with hundreds of gallons of human waste, courtesy of the field latrines.

"You'd better tend to those diapers, whoremaster," the driver taunted.

Ron contained his anger and unloaded the tools. Isaac yanked the water from the tailgate.

"See you later, turds," the foreman yelled as the truck peeled out, showering the boys with grit.

* * *

The noon whistle trumped all other sound. Ron cursed to the sky, "Enough is goddamn enough." He threw his shovel to the ground, brushed dried crap and coke dust from his shoes and went to the union office. Isaac tagged along, not expecting anything more than a long walk and a missed lunch.

After ten minutes of sloughing along paths of mud and dodging potholes filled with rust-colored water, the boys entered a one-story brick building. Besides being the union office, it doubled as a fallout shelter.

"Yeah, what do you want," the receptionist inquired, not looking up from her typewriter.

"I want to file a grievance," Ron said.

"Why," she asked, patting the sides of her beehive hairdo. "Don't you like your workmate?"

Ron squinted. "Excuse me? I need to speak to the shop steward."

"You're Bob Kelly's son, aren't you?"

"Yeah. So what?"

"Maybe you should come back later," she said as she ran blood-red lipstick over her flattened lips.

"What's me being his son got to do with any of this?"

She shrugged. "The steward is awful busy. Maybe your father can help you with your problem."

"That'll be the day."

"He and the steward have been good friends for years,"
she said.

"Listen. I want to see the shop steward not my old man.
When can that happen?"

"Like I said. You'll have to come back. Alone,
preferably." She glanced at Isaac.

"Fuck this place. C'mon, Isaac. Lets get the hell out of
here."

As he turned to leave, an advertisement posted on the
wall caught his eye.

ELECTRICAL TRAINING
SIX-MONTH COURSE
NO TUITION

"How do we sign up," he asked.

"Both of you," she inquired as the smell of coke, sweat
and human waste began to overpower her perfume.

"Who do you think 'we' is? Me and myself and I?" He
pulled Isaac to his side.

"Here," she said, pushing two applications across the
table as if feeding lepers.

"Take 'em but turn 'em in quick. There're only a few
slots."

The boys sat at beat-up school desks and completed the
forms.

"Anything would be better than shoveling shit," Isaac
declared.

"This is serious," Ron said. "I gotta think about my
future."

After twenty minutes, they handed in the applications.

"Here." Isaac slid his to the receptionist.

She handled his papers as if they were dirty underwear,
placing them on the steward's desk.

"When will we hear," Ron asked.

"I'm not sure." She wiped her hands with a tissue. "Class begins later this month. So, a couple of days?"

"I'll check with you later."

"Whatever," she replied as the phone rang.

Isaac elbowed Ron. "Come on. Let's get back before the foreman shows up."

"Wait," she said, her hand over the mouthpiece. "It's the steward."

Ron and Isaac listened to the one-sided conversation. "Yes. He's here. Yes," she looked toward Isaac. "His friend's here, too. They applied for the electrician course. Okay. I'll tell him. See you shortly."

She rested the phone in its cradle. "Looks like you're in luck. The steward, your father and the foreman just finished lunch together. They'll be here in a minute."

"I'm outta here," Isaac said and went for the door.

Ron hesitated. *I can't have a blow up with my old man. Not here. Not with Isaac involved.* "Just make sure you get those applications handed in. Both of them," he said as he and Isaac made a hasty retreat back to the pile of stone.

12.

Katherine spent the morning washing breakfast dishes and tidying the apartment. Near noon she walked out to the third floor landing, hand pressed to her stomach, first surprised then shocked by the wiggle inside.

Bent over and sobbing she cried out, "God, why did you let this happen to me?"

Ben stopped sweeping the sidewalk. He rushed upstairs as fast as his fifty-year-old body could take him.

"Child," he whispered, gasping for air. "What's wrong? Why are you crying?"

She lifted her head. "I'm scared about the future."

"Is that all?" His breathing relaxed. "It'll bring great things, young lady," he said. "You married a fine boy and you're going to raise a fine family some day."

His embrace had no effect as her sobs deepened. "It's okay. You cry. You're just nervous. That's all."

She fought the urge to scream. He pulled a fresh hanky from his back pocket.

"Here," he said. "Use this."

She pushed it away.

He studied her for a moment. "You need something to keep you busy, to keep your mind off of your mind," he said. "How 'bout comin' to work for me in the store?"

"Really," she said, followed by a big swallow. "I've never had a job."

"There's nothing wrong with a woman working. Martha worked before we got married. Heck, she minded the store until Isaac was born. Work's good for the soul."

A sense of calm came over her. "What can I do?"

"I'll find plenty to keep you busy. Freshen up and meet me downstairs in a half hour."

Katherine returned to the apartment, pulled her frenzied hair to a ponytail, washed her face and went through the few clothes hanging in the closet. She picked out a baggy dress. Wearing only panties, she stood in front of the bathroom mirror. Her reflection revealed a small bulge in an otherwise petite waistline.

Oh, God. I'm more pregnant every day.

She didn't bother selecting a belt. The box-cut dress hung wide on her frame.

* * *

Katherine opened the door to a new world. A jingling bell announced her arrival. Wooden crates containing a mélange of outdated items – from frayed horse tack and oxen yolks to fan belts used on steam tractors – lined the walls. The odor of tar and machine oil accompanied her every step. Two fluorescent tubes ran the length of the store, barely enough to light the space

"Come in, come in," Ben said, wiping the counter that displayed power saws, drills and belt sanders.

"Mr. Toony, I hope this old dress is appropriate," she said, absorbing the surroundings.

"Yes, my dear, there's no dress code here," he said. "But you may get a little dirty. Let's find something to keep you clean."

He ducked behind a curtain and returned with a gray cotton smock.

"Here you go. It's not flattering, but it'll keep the dirt off you."

"Oh, I'm not concerned with my figure," she said, pulling the smock over her dress.

Ben removed his visor. He scratched his forehead. "Martha used to wear that thing right up until Isaac was born."

Katherine resembled a walking tee-pee. "I like it just fine. I only wish I had something similar to wear around the apartment when I'm cleaning."

"You can take it with you at the end of the day."

"Really? That'd be great! Thank you."

Ben walked her through the store, explaining what was what and where things went.

As he opened the glass cover protecting his valuable power tools she asked, "Would it be okay if we kept my working here a secret?"

"Why on earth would you want to do that," Ben said.

With the skill of a shyster the words sailed from Katherine's lips. "I want to buy Ron a wedding gift."

Ben smiled. "I don't see any harm in a little white lie," he said. "Sure. I'll let Martha know to keep it quiet. I'll even make sure you're done every day before Ron gets home."

* * *

At the end of the day Ron and Isaac punched their time cards, oblivious to the stink left in their wake. They crossed the main drag, walked to the river and home. Ben had just locked up the store when they arrived.

"Phew," he exclaimed. "Something's rotten in Denmark." He pinched his nose. "I suggest you take those clothes off and leave 'em on the landing. I know two women upstairs who won't want sewer mixin' with dinner."

Isaac stripped to his boxers on the second story landing. Ron did the same on the third.

"Honey," he said as he walked in, "I wanted your sweet ass so bad, I got half-naked on the way home."

Katherine dried her hands on the smock and pinched his cheek.

"What's this thing you're wearin'," Ron joked. "A maternity dress?"

"Don't be silly," she blushed. "It's just something Martha gave me to keep my clothes clean when I'm working around the house. That's all."

"You scared me for a second," he said, giving her a spin in his arms. "We're not ready for kids."

"What do you mean?" Katherine's mind scrambled. *What will he do when he finds out?*

"They're offering free electrician training at the mill. Isaac and me signed up."

She laughed. "Is that so we can have kids?"

"Yeah, but we gotta wait until I get a better job and our own house."

Katherine's mouth gaped. "Do you think we'll get out of this mess, go back to our own part of town?"

"Where our folks live?" Ron smiled. "I don't think so."

He went to the sink, ran cold water and splashed his face. "Listen, honey. I don't plan on staying here forever," he said. "If I pass that test, I'll get you anything you want. Sky's the limit."

Her hands covered her stomach. "Anything?"

"What ever you want, honey."

She walked to the front window, surveying the place they called home. "You're right. It wouldn't be a good idea for us to raise a child in this part of town."

He wiped his face with a dishtowel. "It's not where we live, but how we're living, hiding out like two criminals." He took her in his arms. "But that's going to change."

"How's that gonna happen? You just said–"

"I know what I said. But don't you see? If I get an electrician's license, no one will interfere with me at work. I'll be in a different part of the mill, working with guys who have an education, not the ignorant slobs I'm currently stuck with."

"Yeah, but we still can't move back to Wood Street."

"You ever hear of a car? There're some small houses being built about ten miles or so out of town. I overheard a few guys talking about it. An electrician can afford that type of place."

"You mean a stand-alone house? With a real yard?"

"Like I said, sky's the limit."

He took hold of her hips, but she pulled away.

"What's wrong?" he said.

Silence.

"Do you want me to shower first," he asked between unsuccessful efforts to kiss her.

"What about your father," she asked. "Does he have anything to do with this school thing?"

"Hell no. That's why I want to take this test, so we can get away from guys like him."

Katherine slipped from his arms. Ron snagged her elbow. "What's wrong, baby?"

Her eyes sharpened. "I've heard bad things about him."

"Don't worry. He can't do anything to you," Ron said. "And besides, I'd kill him if he ever laid a hand on you." He stroked her cheek.

"Really?" her voice softened. "You'd do that for me?"

13.

Katherine had worked at the hardware store for a few
weeks. And, with thirty dollars saved, she went to see Ben.
He was cleaning tools in the display case.

"Is something bothering you, child," he said, noticing
her hands clasped and heels grinding the floor.

"Well, Mr. Toony. I have a favor to ask."

He buffed a drill and said, "What can I do for you?"

"I need the day off. I want to visit my mother."

"That's terrific." He tossed the rag aside. "Martha and
me were wondering when you kids would get around to
seein' your folks. Of course you can have the day off." He
came from behind the counter. "You go see your mother.
Let her know you're okay."

Katherine walked toward town. The farther she got from
Toony's, the more determined she became. She began to
trot, her hand covering her stomach. When she hit the main
drag, her pace slowed to a walk, not wanting to draw
attention. Buses, cars and people rushing allowed her to
fold into the morning rhythm. She walked a side street, just
off the town square and entered Averham Bendel's office.
Bendel, a Mennonite, came to town to practice a skill, one
that caused him to be shunned by his orthodox community.

Katherine pulled three ten-dollar bills from her bra cup.
Bendel counted and re-counted. Father Ryan's
admonishment echoed in her head. *There will be no saving
you.*

Bendel handed her a gown. "Here, you need to wear
this."

After he left, she rested her hands on her stomach. She looked at the table, the cold stirrups, the crude instruments and the empty garbage can. She blocked all emotion and began to undress, but the zipper stuck. She twisted and wiggled every which way. No use. It wouldn't come loose. She panicked. Her heart raced. Sweat dripped from her brow and armpits. She spun, tug after tug, until nearly tearing the dress. "I can't do this!" she screamed and bolted from the musty room, past Bendel and into the street. Running and crying her way across town, her instincts brought her to her parents' front porch.

"Mother," she cried. "Mother! Please help me!"

14.

Accustomed to attempts to unseat them, the boys braced their bodies as the truck skidded on the wet dock and came to a halt.

"Out you go, assholes," the foreman commanded. "Check every spike, every rail and shine every turd. Welcome to the whisky train."

The mill's railway stretched for two miles from the river to the open hearth. Each day, freight cars were loaded with coke and limestone, nudged forward until twenty cars, each laden with one hundred and ten tons of cargo, lined the tracks.

Today, as part of their maintenance duties, Ron and Isaac were appointed an inglorious position: trash collectors and rail inspectors.

"I hope you brought your lunch. We won't be back," the driver said, chewing a wad of tobacco.

Isaac muttered, "I hope you choke."

"What'd you say, boy?"

"Okey doke."

"Smart-ass. You'll get yours."

Ron slung a twenty-pound sledge over his shoulder. Isaac strapped a canvas garbage bag to his back. Like two hobos, they walked the railway.

Near the dock, the tracks were clean and sturdy, but as the boys moved farther away debris ranging from porno magazines to spent condoms and empty whiskey bottles dotted the ground.

Ron began to pound loose spikes. Isaac's eyes jolted with every swing. In the weeds he found a cotton pillow, its stuffing a handy earplug. He broke it into puffballs and filled each ear.

About a half mile from the dock, he became used to the racket and picked the cotton from his ears. "When do you think we'll hear about electrician school," he asked.

Ron remained silent, eyes fixed on the rails.

"Yo, Ron," Isaac yelled. "Is anybody home?"

"What the hell you want," Ron shot back.

"Oh. It's the uppity overseer. Sorry, sir," Isaac mocked.

"Don't be a jerk, Isaac. Can't you see something's botherin' me?"

"Like what, Einstein?"

"Don't be funny," he said as he drove another loose spike.

"Okay. If you don't wanna talk about it, just keep acting like I'm not here. I'm used to that around this place anyway."

Ron took another swing. Isaac jumped aside. "Hey, Man. You almost snagged my foot. That was a little too close."

"Sorry."

Isaac tried to grab the sledge. "Gimme that thing before you hurt somebody."

Ron threw the hammer to the ground and sat on the edge of the track, palms shoved to his cheeks.

"What in the hell is with you?" Isaac sat next to him.

Ron tossed a stone into the weeds, but said nothing.

"You want me to guess? Is it the foreman and the driver?"

Ron stared at the weed tops swaying in the breeze.

"Not them, eh? You don't like living in the old part of town? That's it, isn't it?"

Ron shot to his feet. "Fuck off. You know that's not it."

"Well, then what the hell is eatin' you?"

He grabbed the sledge. "Let's get back to work."

"Okay. If that's the way you want it."

They moved along the track. Ron methodically drove spikes while Isaac filled the trash bag. After another hundred yards, the sledge slipped from Ron's hands. "You wanna know what's botherin' me?"

"Only if you wanna tell, brother. I ain't lookin' to pick no fight."

"It's Katherine. Okay. There's something wrong. She's been acting strange ever since I told her about wanting to become an electrician."

"Strange? What kind of strange? Running around the house with a sheet over her head strange?" Isaac laughed.

"Stop fuckin' around, man. It's real and she just feels hollow to me, like there's something goin on."

"I ain't no mind reader and I bet you ain't either," Isaac said. "If you wanna know what's goin on just ask her."

Throughout the morning Ron contemplated Isaac's words. As the boys neared midway on the tracks Ron burst out with, "That's it. You're a fucking genius, Isaac. I'm outta here."

"What the fuck you talkin'?"

Ron handed him the hammer. "Here, take this thing. I don't care if they fire me." His fist pounded his palm. "I've gotta see Katherine. Now!"

"Can't it wait till you get home?"

"You're the one who said just go and ask her."

"Me and my big-ass mouth." Isaac pointed to the horizon. "Go ahead, man. Get the fuck outta here. See if I care."

Ron rested his hand on Isaac's shoulder. "If that asshole foreman shows up you'll cover for me, won't you?"

"What happened to I don't care?"

"Well, I do but I don't. You know what I mean. This shit with Katherine is eatin' me alive. She's up to something. I can feel it when I touch her, when she throws a phony smile as I walk in the door. She even sleeps on the far side of the bed. If I want the truth, I've gotta surprise her. Catch her off guard."

Ron turned to leave, but Isaac took him by the arm. "Hey, man. Promise me one thing will you?"

"What's that?"

"If I ever come around and say I'm gettin' married, just knock me on my ass or something, okay?"

"I owe you one, buddy," Ron said.

He sprinted across an open field toward the chain-link security fence. He wiggled through a hole usually reserved for hookers who serviced night-shift dockworkers. After passing several neon-colored waste lagoons, he cut through a dying forest, and entered the old part of town.

Ben stood in front of the store, shooting the breeze with two workers from Battle Hymn Electric, who had repaired the streetlamp lost to vandalism.

Ron came jogging up. "Hey," he puffed.

"What are you doing here? Where's Isaac?"

"He's cleaning the whiskey train. I have to speak with Katherine. She upstairs?"

"No. She's gone to visit her mother, something you should consider."

"Thanks," he said, not breaking stride as he headed toward Wood Street.

* * *

Though lost in last night's drunken fog, Bob Kelly swigged whisky like water as he swung the crane between the barge and the hopper. With the coke barge empty, he shifted the crane into gear and rolled to the limestone. Longshoremen took their time opening the cargo hold so he took advantage of his one-hundred-foot perch, noticing a lone black man walking the tracks.

It's that jungle bunny, he thought and called Duffy on the radio. "Listen, pal," he whispered, "get the field glasses and look toward the tracks. There's someone out there."

"Oh, yeah. I see him. Who is the son bitch?"

"It's the darkie who's been interfering with me and my family." Kelly said. "And he's all alone. He'll probably be there most of the day."

"What's up your sleeve?"

"You'll see."

* * *

Mrs. O'Hara sat with her daughter on the couch, attempting to assuage her anguish. "It's okay, darling. Don't cry. Your mother's here."

Katherine wailed.

"What's troubling you?"

"I'm...I." Katherine clung to her mother. "I'm going to have a baby."

"Well, that's something, now, isn't it? I've been waiting for you to tell me." Mrs. O'Hara's calm stunned her daughter. "You think you're the only girl to get pregnant out of wedlock? Don't kid yourself. You made a mistake, but you corrected it. You're married."

"But, but Mother, you don't understand," Katherine pleaded, her moment of truth at hand.

"Oh, I don't, do I?" She patted her daughter's hair. "Let me guess. Ron doesn't know?"

There was a long silence.

I can't tell her. If Kelly doesn't kill her, the truth will.

"That's right," Katherine said. "He doesn't know."

"Everything is fine with you physically?"

"Yes, I'm fine, in that way."

"Well, then. It's simple. Tell your Ronald he's going to be a father."

"He told me he didn't want to have children right away."

"That's what he says now, but trust me. Like all men, when you mention 'baby,' he'll treat you like an egg. It'll drive you mad."

Katherine sniffled. "What if he gets mad?"

"Nonsense. He's not that kind of boy." She pulled Katherine to her. "You're going to have a child. My grandchild."

Footsteps and heavy breathing on the front porch interrupted their embrace. Mrs. O'Hara left Katherine on the couch and peered through a side curtain. *What in God's name is he doing here?*

* * *

Blue Mountain's silhouette gobbled the sun. Isaac tossed another whiskey bottle in the sack. "Number twenty," he said and looked at his watch. *Thirty minutes till quittin' time.* He pounded the last spike of the day. The sound of tires crunching gravel grew louder. Over his shoulder, a truck kicking up a plume of dust headed his way. He struggled to come up with some last-minute excuse to explain Ron's absence. The pick-up downshifted and skidded to a stop. A new driver hung his tattooed arms over the steering wheel.

"Your name Toony?"

"Who wants to know?"

"Listen, boy. Don't get angry with me. I'm just delivering the message."

"What message?"

"The foreman wants to see you. It's somethin' about going to school or some shit like that."

Isaac permitted a smile on his face. "Why didn't you say so," he said, preparing to toss the sack of garbage and sledge in the truck bed.

"Nah, leave that shit," the driver said. "It'll help you know where to start tomorrow. C'mon, get in."

"Okay," Isaac said and went to hop in the back of the truck.

"Sit up front, son," the driver offered.

Preoccupied with promises of the future, he took a seat in the cab. The driver swung the truck around and sped back to the dock.

"Here we are." He grinned, his gums tarred with chewing tobacco.

"Hey wait," Isaac said. "The office is farther down the rails."

"I gotta get to the maintenance shed, boy. Get your black ass out of my truck."

Isaac threw the driver a sideways glance while exiting. The guy popped the clutch and took off.

The 4:00 p.m. whistle sounded the end to another day, and as usual, dockworkers had left fifteen minutes early. The second shift would arrive in thirty minutes.

Isaac walked the rails leading to the hopper office. There was no sign of the foreman or anybody else for that matter. The cranes and hoists stood idle. The place was a ghost town.

"Hey, foreman," he bellowed. "It's Isaac Toony. Where are you?" His voice echoed off the iron hull of a barge and sheet metal warehouse.

Two hundred yards away, a lone figure emerged from the office, signaling with a sweeping arm gesture.

"Ron," Isaac shouted, "Hey. Is that you?"

The person was saying something, but Isaac couldn't make out what. As he neared the office, goosebumps sprouted over every inch of his body when he realized the person coming toward him wasn't Ron or offering a friendly gesture. The man began to jog.

Oh fuck, it's him, Isaac thought as the man moved closer.

The guy flipped the middle finger and jabbed his arm to the sky. "Look up, boy," he shouted. "Ya just won a trip to darkie heaven."

Isaac looked up as the hopper opened and the sky turned black, raining one hundred and ten tons of coke. He jumped, trying to avoid the falling chunks, but the first blast caught his head. The rest of his body followed his shattered skull, pummeled to the rails. Only his twitching feet protruded from beneath the dusty mountain of death.

15.

"You have so much to look forward to," Mrs. O'Hara said as the trio stood on the front porch. Ron and Katherine held hands.

Mrs. O'Hara turned to him. "And you. This is my daughter and that baby will be my grandchild. Don't let anything happen to them. Promise."

"Katherine means everything to me," Ron said. "I didn't mean to sound so upset in the living room. I'm sorry. But now that I know what's been bothering her...I thought she was cheating on me" He kissed her forehead. "Don't worry. I'll take good care of her. And you can tell her father I said so."

"Don't tell Daddy about the baby," Katherine said. "I'll let him know in a few weeks, in my own way."

"Haven't you hid enough from the poor man, a surprise wedding, living with the coloreds? Give him something to be happy about. Remember what I told you about men and babies? It applies to grandfathers as well as fathers."

"Please don't say anything."

"You're as pigheaded as ever."

Katherine gave her a steely look.

"Oh, all right. I won't tell him." She looked at Ron. "How about you? Are you going to tell your folks about becoming grandparents? It might change your father's tune."

"I doubt that."

Katherine put her hands to her head. "We have to go now," she said. "I have meat thawing on the counter."

"Okay, my little mother-to-be. Have a good supper."

Ron supported her down the steps. "Honey, are you all right. Should we get a cab? Do you need to lay down?"

Katherine looked over her shoulder at her mother, who remained silent but with eyes that said, *He'll treat you like an egg. It'll drive you mad.*

"No, Ron, I can walk. Let's get out of here."

On the next block they paused in front of the Kelly's house.

"What are you doing, Ron?"

"Let's tell my mom. She'll be so happy."

He pulled on her arm, but she wouldn't budge.

"I'm not going up there."

The 4:00 p.m. whistle blew its message.

"What's the big deal?" Ron scrunched his shoulders.

"I'm not going and that's that!"

"Okay. Okay. You wait here. I tell her myself."

She heard him yell "Ma, where are you?" as he wandered the house.

On the sidewalk, she looked around as though someone might sneak up on her.

Ron jumped from the porch. "Nobody's here. She's at the market or something."

"Get me home," Katherine said, holding her stomach. "I'm hungry."

A high-pitched siren stopped them, the first blast followed by three short bursts.

"There's been an accident at the mill," he said.

After a few minutes, they approached the hardware store, the blinds drawn and lights out. "That's strange. Mr. Toony usually keeps its open an extra half hour on Fridays."

The Toony apartment looked empty.

"The car's gone," Ron said.

"Maybe they're having a night out?"

"Why don't we have a night in?" He nuzzled her ear

"You don't waste any time, do you?"

"Not when it comes to gettin' in the sack with you."

"You know, it's not good for pregnant women to have sex. You might hurt the baby."

"Where'd you hear a crazy thing like that, in church?"

"No. As a matter of fact, I read it in *Reader's Digest.*"

"Really? You mean no sex until the baby's born?"

"That's what the article said."

"But there's other types of sex."

She slapped his face. "How dare you? You think I'm a whore or something?"

She read the hurt in his eyes. Not physical pain, but the type that strikes a man's pride. "I'm sorry, Ron. I didn't mean to do that."

"It's okay. I understand. We're in a tough spot and now it's tougher."

His hand rested against her cheek.

* * *

The morning brought hushed voices accented by cries of agony. Ron slipped into a pair of boxers and went to the window. His old-town neighbors milled restlessly on the sidewalk. They started toward downtown, but a minister broke from the group, hands raised.

"Wait. Give these folks their day of peace," he begged. His power of common sense halted whatever was about to take place as the group drew around him. He bowed his head, blessed the crowd, and ascended the stairs. Ron heard Ben answer the door, the minister's soothing condolence and Martha's primal scream.

He returned to the bedroom. Katherine, wearing a white nightgown, eased to a standing position.

"What's going on down there, Ron?"

"There's a problem or something. Martha sounds like she's ready to die."

He combed his unruly hair and got dressed. "I'm going downstairs."

People in the street gave him a cold stare. He watched his back and tapped the window before entering the Toony's apartment. Martha, prostrate on the couch, cried into a pillow, the minister at her side.

"There, there, my dear" he said. "It'll be okay. The boy was called home to Jesus and someday you'll be with him." The shiny-headed preacher stroked her hair. "It was his time. That's all. It was just his time."

Ben stood over them, a handkerchief pushed to his eyes.

"Excuse me, but what's wrong," Ron asked.

Ben raised his head and scratched his bald spot, trying to control his emotions. "It's Isaac. He was crushed to death. They say it was a load of coke that broke loose from a hopper." He gritted his teeth. "I think somebody dumped that stone on my boy."

"Isaac? Dead? How could it…when?" *My old man told me King Kong couldn't break the seal of a hopper.*

"It happened sometime between the shift change," Ben cursed. "One of the longshoremen found him."

Ron's eyes filled with tears as he approached Martha, but Ben grabbed him by the arm with such force that he almost fell.

"Not now, son. Are you blind? Can't you see the woman's lost in grief?"

Ron pinched his eyes as Ben nearly shoved him out the door.

"We need to be alone."

16.

After they buried Isaac, Martha and Ben stayed with family for a few days before returning home. On their first day back, Katherine, wearing her smock, greeted Ben in the front of the store. "I'm sorry about Isaac," she said.

Ben collected a pile of morning papers that had gone unread during his absence, and unlocked the door. "Thank you, child," he muttered. His eyes caught the bump in her smock. "You on the nest?"

"Yes," she said, her cheeks flushed.

"Well, I guess it's a good thing."

"What do you mean you guess?"

"Bring a child into this world? I don't know anymore. Things aren't the same."

Katherine's head tilted down. "You mean Isaac and all?"

"My boy will be forgotten as a soldier in a tiny skirmish. There's a big war comin'."

The words floated right by Katherine's ears as she began to enter the store. Ben blocked the way with his size eleven shoe. "Unless you're here to buy something, I can't help you."

Stunned, Katherine asked, "I'm here to work. You know that."

"You innocent young woman. You can't work here anymore."

"Why? I didn't do anything."

"Like I said, *things* are different." He put his hand on her shoulder, his voice almost a whisper, "There are some people who won't welcome white people in this part of town." He surveyed the surroundings.

For the first time, Katherine felt like an outsider. "Who'd wanna hurt me?"

"It's not you so much as it is Ron. People say he should've stayed with Isaac instead of runnin' off in the middle of the day." Ben fumbled with the damp, brownish newspapers, almost dropping them. "Some folks think he was in on it, making sure nobody else took his spot in electrician school. Heck. Even I was rude to him when he came to the house to pay his respects because all I saw was a white man."

He turned to enter the store, Katherine grabbing at his shirtsleeves.

"Mr. Toony. Ron would have never done anything to harm your son. Isaac was the best friend he had."

"I know. I realize that now. But there's a group who think the fruit don't fall far from the tree," he said, looking toward the burned-out Davis store. "I think you and Ron better find another place to live," he continued. "I don't want you to get hurt and I don't want Ron's people comin' here to mess with me and Martha."

He broke Katherine's grip. "And besides," he said, "I'm closing the store for a while."

"Why? Where you going?"

"Martha and me are headed to Birmingham, Alabama."

"What on earth for?"

"You wouldn't understand," he said. He left her with, "Get outta here for your own good." Then he went into the store, throwing the deadbolt behind him.

* * *

On the first day of electrician school, the egg-shaped instructor informed all students they would be relegated to sweeping floors and emptying trash in the corporate building after class. Two hours later, mops and brooms were dispensed.

As Ron skimmed dust with a six-foot mop, he left behind a trail of high-shined linoleum. The object of this job was to dodge button-down managers and move from one corridor to another. Unchallenged, his mind flooded with thoughts of Isaac and the faulty hopper. He recreated the scene expecting a different outcome, but Isaac always ended up dead.

It had to be my old man.

When the whistle sounded, he ran from the building. A long line of second-shift workers formed at the security gate. In the confusion, he passed Mr. O'Hara unnoticed. But as he headed home a roar of laughter came from the crowd. He turned, recognizing the loudest voice. His father, surrounded by the usual group, formed a finger pistol and pointed toward O'Hara.

"Bang!"

"Oh, you got me," Duffy hollered and the crowd roared again.

Ron blended with people going to their cars, wanting to avoid his father for fear of what might happen. At a safe distance, he broke from the group.

When he arrived home, the hardware store was dark. He climbed the stairs, anxious and hungry. Midway, Martha came out to the second story landing. She looked at him, retreated to her apartment, and drew the blinds.

What's that about, he wondered, entering his place to find Katherine stacking clothes and their few belongings on the bed.

"You cleaning closets," he asked.

"No." She didn't break stride.

"Where can a guy get something to eat?"

"Not here."

"How 'bout we go to Gerber's for dinner?"

"How 'bout you help me get our stuff packed?"

Ron took her arm. "Whoa," he said. "Packed? Where we goin'?"

She brushed hair from her eyes and wiped her runny nose with the back of her hand.

"We've been kicked out. Mr. Toony wants us to leave."

"Wait, Katherine. Are you sure you didn't misunderstand?"

He sat on the bed and pulled her to his lap. Katherine reiterated Ben's request.

"How can he think I had anything to do with it?" Ron said.

"I told you, it's not him. It's other people in the neighborhood who don't like us. We're not safe here."

"You hang on," he said. "I'll be right back."

He knocked on Ben's door. No response. He knocked harder, almost cracking the glass. Ben stepped onto the landing. "I know what you want," he said, Martha's sobs in the background.

"Why," Ron asked. "I thought there was something special here, something that rose above the crap Katherine and me ran away from."

"There's things in play that are bigger than us, son."

"Where can we go? You can't just give us the boot."

"Martha and me are leavin' for Alabama. We'll be gone for a while." Ben pulled Ron close. "For the love of God, boy, and for both our safety, get outta here before we get back."

He purposely donned his glasses, enhancing the roadmap of red veins traversing his yellowish eyeballs. "I know you had nothing to do with Isaac's death. But things are going to get hot around here. Summer could be a tippin'

point in this town. Get out while you can. Protect your wife
and your baby. Find another place."

Disappointed, Ron returned to the apartment, Katherine
still packing.

"Hold on, hold on," he said. "We've got a week. Let's
think this through."

"I'm afraid, Ron. We'd better go before your father or
some of the colored people cause trouble."

Ron slammed his foot to the floor. "I need time, damn
it! I need some goddamn time!" He sunk to the floor and
drew his knees to his chest. Katherine slid down beside
him. "I just want to a better life." His voice cracked and he
buried his head in his arms.

"Me too, that's all I ever wanted," she said, resting her
head on his shoulder.

He raised his chin. "I'll find us a place, something to
hold us over 'til I get my electrician's license."

They moved their belongings from the bed to the closet,
and walked to Gerber's.

* * *

Gerber's counter had a smattering of customers. Ron and
Katherine plopped on the same stools as the night before
their wedding. Their glum faces reflected in the wall
mirror. She twirled egg noodles with a fork while he
nudged a burger around the greasy plate.

After several minutes of silence, he closed his eyes and
rested his head on the edge of the counter. Katherine ran
her fingers through his hair. While doing so, she heard a
faint tap on the front window. At first glance, through the
metal tree of greeting cards, she barely noticed a face
pushed to the glass. A second take brought a blood-curdling
scream. She slid from her stool. Ron's quick reaction

caught her head before it smashed to the floor. Other dinner patrons gathered, murmuring their concern.

"Katherine, Katherine, what is it?"

She grunted and opened her eyes.

"Is it the baby," he asked.

Ron looked into her terror-filled eyes. She clutched his arm, almost breaking skin.

"It's him," she cried, looking toward the window.

All eyes followed her glare. There was nothing but foot traffic and cars passing.

"Who was it?"

Katherine studied the faces that silently questioned her.

"It was…"

"Tell me, Katherine."

"It was your father!"

The soda jerk knelt beside them.

"Here," Ron said. "Hold her head for a moment."

He ran from the store, searching one direction then another. After covering a city block, he returned to Gerber's. Now seated in a booth, Katherine sipped water through a straw. Ron sat next to her.

"I didn't see him," he said. "Are you sure it was my father?"

"I, I'm almost positive."

"There're a lot of drunks in Battle Hymn."

"I'm so embarrassed," she said, shrinking in her seat.

"No need to be. You're pregnant. People will think you had a hot flash or somethin'."

Katherine finished the water. Ron looked out the window.

"Do you have enough strength to walk home," he asked.

"I think so."

He dropped a five-dollar bill on the counter. The soda jerk poured fresh syrup into a soda dispenser. "Need any change," he asked.

"No," Ron said as he supported Katherine with an arm around her waist.

"Okay, thanks," said the jerk.

The couple walked toward the hardware store. Soon, only a handful of streetlamps lit the way. As they turned onto their block, Ron stopped and spun around.

"What is it?" Katherine was on the verge of panic.

"I thought I heard footsteps."

They walked faster, the street pure darkness because the recently repaired streetlamp had been broken again.

"It doesn't look like Ben and Martha are awake," he said. They tiptoed up the steps. On the landing, she stubbed her foot on something. Ron bent down and felt his way to a rock. Underneath it was a piece of crumpled paper.

After they entered the apartment, he bolted the door and flipped the light switch. He flattened the paper on the counter. Katherine began to scream, but Ron cupped her mouth with his hand and read the message scrawled in black crayon.

U R NEXT

17.

A revving engine and headlamps woke Ron. He carefully untangled himself from Katherine's arms, slipping from bed unnoticed. Not long after, Katherine stirred. She came to the window naked, sprouting a fresh crop of goose bumps. They watched as the DeSoto disappeared around the bend.

"They're off to Alabama," she said.

"I hope the clunker makes it," he added.

They sat in the kitchen, the crumpled note facing them.

"Get dressed then pack your stuff," he commanded.

"What are we going to do?"

"We're leaving. Now!"

"Where to? What about work?"

"I'm calling in sick. We've gotta find a new place to live."

Out came the suitcases. Katherine packed clothes and toiletries. Frightened, angry and confused, she began to lock her suitcase, but stopped and opened the lid. She removed an article of clothing.

"Come on," Ron said. "I've got to get to Gerber's and phone the personnel office before my shift begins."

"Just a second, Ron. I don't want to leave the place looking like a disaster."

Katherine straightened the sheets, fluffed the pillows and tightened the bedspread. Ron locked the suitcase.

"What's that you're holding," he asked.

"It's something I borrowed but I don't need anymore."

"Okay, then leave it. Hurry up."

Ron grabbed the luggage and stood at the door, holding it open with his foot. Katherine folded the smock, placed it on a pillow, and looked around the small space. She wanted to wipe her memory of Martha, Ben and Isaac, but she couldn't.

"C'mon," Ron said.

The wind caught the door and slammed it shut behind them as they scurried down the stairs.

* * *

Ron stopped pacing and stood inches from the phone booth, hoping to drive the man inside away. The door flew open.

"You don't have to hover, buddy. I'm done."

"Sorry. But I have to call work before the whistle blows." He popped a dime in the slot and called personnel. After the call ended, he emerged relieved and joined Katherine at the counter.

"Is everything okay?" she asked.

"No problem. They gave me the day off."

As they ate, Ron thought of every apartment building or boarding house nearby.

After breakfast, they caught a taxi and drove to various sites, only to be told, "Nah, nothing available."

The taxi driver sized up the dejected youngsters slumped in his backseat. "You two look like the world's against you," he said.

"Not the world," Ron replied. "Just this town."

"I know a place where you can stay. It isn't much, but it's a roof and it's clean."

"Is it near the mill," Ron asked. "I don't have a car."

"It's just outside the truck entrance on the far side of the mill. Maybe you can hitch a ride to work with some of the truckers."

Katherine winced, recalling how her father referred to truckers as "dirty roughnecks."

"What's it called," Ron asked.

"You probably never heard of it. It had no name, that is, until a new owner fixed it up."

The driver put the car in gear and drove to the far side of the mill on a desolate stretch of old highway lined by weeds, garbage and frayed slices of recapped tires.

Twenty minutes later, the cab rolled to a stop in front of a brick diner with a picture window that ran the length of the building.

In the parking lot, mounted on top of a fifty-foot pole sat a large four-leaf clover. On its face: the name of the establishment written in fancy white script. Flatbed trucks loaded and empty parked roadside, engines idling. Choking diesel fumes filled the air.

"Where are the rooms," Katherine inquired, nudging Ron aside in order to check the place out.

"There's no rooms," the cabbie replied. "The new owner fixed up some old cabins in the back. I think there's eight of 'em."

Ron squeezed Katherine's hand. "Wait here, honey. I'll see what the deal is."

When he entered the diner, banging dishes and food orders being called to a short-order cook replaced the rumble of truck motors. The lunch counter was three times the length of Gerber's. The smell of home cooking overpowered the diesel-laden jumpsuits worn by most of the customers.

Hands shoved in his pockets, Ron waited in line while a very large, muscular man wearing a tee shirt with USMC emblazoned on the chest dipped an ice cream cone for a tubby trucker.

"That's fifteen cents," the man said, passing the three-scoop cone of chocolate to his happy customer.

"Next?"

The trucker gazed at his treat. He didn't notice Ron, who did a quick side step to the counter.

"What can I do you for," the man joked.

"I hear you got some rooms for rent," Ron said.

The man looked past Ron and to the waiting taxi.

"Yeah. I've got a cabin that's available. Is it just you?"

"I've got my wife. She's expecting."

"Not here I hope," the man said as he wiped spilt drips of ice cream.

"She's not due for a while," Ron replied, resting his sweaty palms on the clean counter.

"You work?"

"I'm in electrician school at the mill. I'll have my license in the fall."

The man produced a black book. "Here. Find a blank page and give me the basics."

When Ron finished he asked, "How much?"

The man smiled. "I knew you were desperate because that wasn't your first question."

He perused Ron's registration.

"You probably don't earn much, so I won't take advantage," he said. "It's four dollars a day, including fresh sheets, towels and breakfast."

Ron did silent math. *Twenty-eight a week, I earn forty-five.*

"I'll take it."

"Okay. Have the driver pull to cabin six. I'll send one of the kitchen guys around with the key and your linen."

As Ron turned to leave, the man's large hand clamped down on his shoulder. "That'll be eight dollars in advance. I don't like being mean, but I hate being stupid."

Ron handed him twenty-eight dollars.

"This is for the week. I'll pay up every Friday."

"I guess a week makes us neighbors. Welcome to The Cloverleaf. Joe Geary's my name."

"Ron Kelly. I'll bring my wife around after we get settled."

18.

Mrs. Kelly searched the house, desperate for the slip of paper with Ron's phone number. Finally, she went to the bedroom and there on the dresser, she found it half-hidden under an ashtray.

How'd it get here?

She dialed and listened with anticipation as each ring went unanswered, hoping the next sound would be Ron's voice. After twenty rings, she hung up. She heard Mrs. Magee move her listening cup on the other side of the wall. She went next door and knocked.

"Oh, how are you, Margaret," Mrs. Magee inquired. "Won't you come in for a chat?"

The women sat on a burgundy sofa lined with a white antimacassar. White doilies protected the wooden end tables from the assault of tarnished metal lamps.

"I haven't seen you for a while," Mrs. Magee began. "Your husband isn't trifling with you again, is he?"

"No. He's not given me a nasty glance. I believe Ronald put the fear of God in him."

"That won't last," Magee assured, digging at her underarm. "You know, I still have that phone number if you need it."

"Well, it's funny you say that. I tried to call but there was no answer. I thought maybe I had the wrong number. Can I see your copy?"

"Wait here. I have it posted in the back room." She trundled to the kitchen and back. "Here it is. Let's compare notes."

The women drew together, producing eyeglasses from apron pockets.

"They're the same," Mrs. Kelly confirmed. "Is your phone working?"

"Help yourself."

Mrs. Kelly went to the kitchen, dialed, and after many rings, hung up. She returned to the front room and sat next to Mrs. Magee.

"No answer," she said. "I wonder where their place is."

"Let me see that thing." Mrs. Magee grabbed the paper. "Ah. Look here. You see the first three numbers? Darkie Town. That's where this exchange is."

"How ya know that?"

She produced a slim phonebook from the end table drawer.

"This thing tells you who's who and where they are."

Mrs. Magee's finger slid down the page. "No," she said. "Not the colored funeral home."

On the next page, in the middle of her skim, she stopped and tapped the book.

"Here it is, just as I thought. It's that old hardware store. That's the place."

"Stupid kid," Mrs. Kelly sighed. "My boy knows better than to be living with the blacks."

"Tough luck for him," Mrs. Magee shrugged. "Your husband will kill him when he finds out."

"But he doesn't know," Mrs. Kelly said. She recalled finding the phone number under the ashtray.

"Sorry to leave so soon, Mrs. Magee, but it's an emergency. I gotta get somewhere, quick."

* * *

In front of Toony's, children played jump rope and hopscotch on the sidewalk as Mrs. Kelly approached. "Excuse me, kids," she said. "I'm looking for someone."

"He a white boy," one of the girls asked while double-dutching.

Mrs. Kelly looked around to see if any adults were watching. "Yeah, he is."

One of the other little girls interrupted. "I know who he is. I know him. He was Isaac's friend."

"Who's Isaac," Mrs. Kelly inquired.

"Isaac Toony. You know, the boy who got killed."

"I never heard about that. Where'd he live?"

The little girl turned and pointed to the flat above the hardware store.

"Up there," she said, "and the white boy lives on the top floor with his girlfriend."

"They still there," Mrs. Kelly asked.

"I dunno."

"Thank you, kids."

She walked to the third floor, and after several knocks she gave the handle a try. The door squeaked open. There was no sign of her son or Katherine, only a crumpled piece of paper on the kitchen table and a smock on the foldout bed. Again, she looked around as though someone might be watching. Satisfied she was alone, she slowly unfolded the paper. *This looks like Bob's scrawl.*

Back on the sidewalk, she tried the door to the store.

"They ain't there," one of the girls shouted.

Startled, Mrs. Kelly walked to the youngsters.

"Where'd they go?"

"I think they sick or somethin'."

"Why do you say that?"

"Momma say they went to visit Dr. King."

19.

Joe Geary stood at the base of his sign. His eyes traced the fifty-foot tall gamble as he flipped a switch and the giant cloverleaf lit up, a green halo in the sky. The sudden burst of light gave luminous touches to the brick diner and soot-covered trucks.

Ron and Katherine, rested and all moved in, stood in awe.

"It looks like a beacon," Ron said.

"I hope so," Geary replied. "If it ain't, I'm sunk."

Katherine wore a skimpy top and stretch pants, her naval partially exposed. Geary eyeballed her head to toe.

"Your husband said you're expecting."

She shrugged, slightly embarrassed.

"When are you due?"

Like an excited kid, Ron interjected. "Sometime around Christmas."

"That tummy looks mighty big. Perhaps there're twins in there." Geary joked.

"How can you tell," Ron asked.

"Long story short? My dad was the only doctor in town. He used to drag me to the farms. He delivered most of the babies. I was gonna be a doctor, but when the war came along, well… everything changed. I was a corpsman assigned to a Marine platoon. In the Pacific, we won ground one village at a time. Along the way, I learned about death and delivered a few babies."

Katherine touched her abdomen, her eyes fixed on the ground.

"Oh, I'm sorry, young lady. I've upset you. That's rude of me."

"It's okay," Katherine replied.

"Well," Geary said, trying to shift gears, "since you didn't have the free breakfast, the dinner's on me." He stood between the couple. His muscular frame was two times that of Ron's. "Let's feed however many babies you got," he said.

Geary took an instant liking to his new tenants. They were young and innocent looking. Not the fly-by-night trucker type. He ushered them to a corner booth.

"Here you go, kids. Sit in my private seat."

Ron and Katherine ordered turkey with all the fixings, after which they devoured a slice of apple pie. Geary came to the booth, hands on hips.

"Now, when's the last time you tasted that kind of home cooking," he asked.

"When I lived at home," Ron said.

"How long ago was that?"

Katherine wiped crust from her lips. "It seems like a lifetime."

Geary rubbed the back of his neck. "Why are nice kids like you staying in a roadside motel? Are you from Battle Hymn?"

The couple nodded.

"Where are your families?"

Neither offered a response.

"I guess it's none of my business," Geary said. "But as long as you're here, you can call the Cloverleaf home."

"Thanks," Ron said.

A waitress cleared the table as Geary turned to leave.

"Mr. Geary," Ron called out. "Is there anybody who can give me a lift to the mill in the morning? I don't have a car."

Geary paused, searching his brain for an answer. He clicked his finger. "You can hitch a ride with Lenny the milkman. He stops here before heading to the commissary."

"Thanks again, Mr. Geary."

"No sweat, kid. See you in the morning."

They returned to their one-room cabin. Ron unfolded the couch and stretched out. Katherine sat on a hardwood chair, staring at pine paneling, tapping her feet on the red linoleum. She fidgeted until Ron shouted, "Can you cool it? That noise is making me nuts."

She retreated to the bathroom – nothing more than a closet with a sink, toilet and shower – and closed the door. Ron heard her sobs mix with running the water.

"I'm sorry," he said, standing outside the plywood door. "I'm nervous about that note we found."

Katherine opened the door, eyes dripping.

"Maybe I should go home, Ron?"

"What are you talking about? We're in this together."

"After what happened to Isaac," she cried, "I'm afraid. But if we split up no one will bother us."

"You think things will be better for you back on Wood Street? Don't kid yourself. You walking around as big as a blimp and no husband?"

He wrapped her in his arms. "Your place is with me," he assured, kissing her forehead. "We only have to stick it out a few more months. When I graduate school, I'll get a car and we can find a place."

"But what about your father," she sniffled.

"Let me worry about him. You take care of that kid."

20.

Mrs. O'Hara lifted the receiver, her tone saccharine, her face perturbed. "Oh yes. He's right here." She cupped the mouthpiece. "It's your boss, Captain Sullivan."

Sullivan's voice boomed. O'Hara held the receiver two feet from his ear.

"Johnny boy," Sullivan began. "I'll be needin' to move you from the front guardhouse to the ass end of the mill."

"Why's that, Captain?"

"Well, one manager decided to drive out there and go through the trucking security gate today. I guess he wanted to check on things. But wouldn't you know it. Old Shamus was sleeping on the job. It seems someone slipped him a bottle. I put the poor geezer on administrative leave until the white-collar boys cool down."

"No problem, Captain. You can count on me."

"I knew I could, Johnny. By the way, you can pick up Shamus' squad car at the main building. It's yours to use, lad. Oh, I almost forgot. How's the problem with your daughter?"

"We're adjusting. It takes time."

"I'll offer a prayer for you." He hacked into the phone. "Be at the truck gate before seven in case one of those pain-in-the-ass managers comes snooping."

O'Hara rested the phone in its cradle. "The truck gate," he sighed. "If fumes don't knock you out, boredom will."

Mrs. O'Hara prepared two plates. "Sit, John. Let's eat."

He offered a dinner prayer then dug in. Halfway through the meal, his knife and fork dropped to the table as if he'd lost all strength.

"What is it, John?"

"It's Katherine," he replied.

"What about her?"

"I'm not coming around, mind you. But I'm worried." He pushed fish with his pinky. "Ever since the Toony boy died, I feel guilty. Like I might have been able to prevent it."

"Nonsense." Her flatware smacked the table. "There was a complete and thorough investigation. That poor colored boy was in the wrong place at the wrong time."

"Yeah, but there's still a lot of jabber about murder. A lot of people say a Kelly did it."

"Surely you don't think Ron would be involved something like that?"

"What I think isn't important. It's what the coloreds think. That's what threatens our daughter." He got up from the table and went to the phone.

"Who are you calling?"

"They're in the old part of town, above a hardware store, right?"

"Yes."

"I want to see how they're doing."

He found Toony's number in the phone book. After a minute of rings, he dropped the phone onto the counter.

"Maybe they're out," she suggested.

"Tomorrow I'll use the squad car and pay Katherine a visit during lunch."

"That'd be wonderful," she said. "You'll call me afterwards?"

"Of course I will, love."

* * *

Ron waited outside the diner, catching a quick smoke, Katherine at his side. The time: 5:45 a.m. and the place hummed. Truck drivers occupied every stool and booth. Geary manned the cash register. He looked out the diner's picture window and waved Ron and Katherine in, pointing to his private seat. Ron snuffed his cigarette. He and Katherine took Geary up on his offer. As they sat, a large refrigerator van entered the parking lot, a picture of two mules pulling a Conestoga wagon painted on its panels.

"This must be my ride," Ron said, head tilted toward the van.

"But you didn't get a chance to eat."

"I'll grab something later."

They watched as Lenny the milkman unloaded two cases of white milk, one of chocolate, a case of orange juice and a tray containing five-dozen eggs. He stacked the provisions on a hand truck, which he then wheeled through the front door.

"Hey, Joe, same place," he asked, his finger pointed toward the kitchen.

"Yeah," Geary replied. "The cook will do the check-in."

Ron came to the cash register. "Is this my ride?"

Geary, counting change, replied, "Yeah. Wait a minute and I'll talk to him."

After a few minutes passed, Lenny came from the kitchen, stopping at the cash register to give Geary a bill. "See you tomorrow, Joe."

"Hey, before you go, can you do me favor?"

"Sure, if I can."

Geary waved Ron over. "My friend here and his wife will be staying with me for a few weeks." He motioned for Katherine to also come to the counter.

"As you can see, the missus is in the family way."

Katherine offered a sweet smile.

"Well, what can I do for ya?"

"Ron doesn't have a car and he'll be needin' a lift to the mill each morning while he's attending class. Can ya give him a ride?"

Ron interjected, "I'll pay, if that makes any difference."

Lenny waved his hand. "No. No. Keep your dough."

"But I don't like to freeload," Ron insisted.

Lenny, a pencil-thin black man of sixty with hazy blue eyes, gave him a quick head-to-toe.

"When's your class?" he asked.

"It starts at eight."

"Is it in the main building near the front gate?"

"Yeah."

Lenny removed his cap and buffed the patent leather bill with his scrawny forearm.

"I'll tell you what. The commissary is in the main building. You can help me unload their delivery before you go to school. How's that?"

"Great," Ron replied, his arm intertwined with Katherine's.

"There you go," Geary said. "You're all set."

Ron and Lenny hopped in the van and drove toward the truck entrance.

After putting away two stacks of buttermilk pancakes, Katherine sat long-faced on a stool near the cash register.

"What's the puss for, young lady?" Geary inquired.

"I dunno. I guess I'll go back to the cabin."

"What are you gonna do all day?"

"Stare at the walls, stare at my stomach. I dunno."

"Since you and your man are obviously on a budget, how'd you like to earn yourselves free dinner?"

"Doing what?" Katherine asked.

Geary's muscular arm waved across the diner. "There's only one of me. When it gets busy I could use some help on the register." He slid a stool from under the counter. "You can sit on this thing so you don't wear out your tootsies."

"I've never run a cash register," Katherine admitted, perplexed by rows of red, yellow and orange buttons.

"Come here. I'll show you. It's easy."

Between serving customers, Geary reviewed the machine's functions, after which he pretended to be a customer. Katherine pushed buttons, rang up the bill and made change like a pro.

"See," Geary said. "If I can do it, anybody can."

Katherine smiled and took up her new position.

"You're missing something," Geary said. He reached in a box under the counter and produced a blank nametag. "How do you spell it? With a 'C' or 'K'?"

"With a 'K'."

She pinned the tag to her blouse, waiting for her first customer. Geary returned to the kitchen to help crank out food orders.

21.

O'Hara parked his squad car in the gravel lot. He walked across the outbound lane, waved to the outbound guard and joined Officer Terry Hanson, who was checking the IDs of incoming truckers.

"You're an hour early, O'Hara, thank God," Hanson said.

"Just wanted to get a feel for the place," he replied, surveying the shanty, its lone telephone pole and single wire connecting the guards to the outside world.

"Well, I feel as though I've been on duty a lifetime," Hanson said, returning an ID to a restless trucker, who pulled away from the guardhouse. The flatbed spewed black exhaust like a rolling volcano. Hanson fidgeted, grabbing his crotch. "Would you mind, O'Hara?"

"Shoot."

"That's exactly what I've gotta do. Shoot me a stream. I'll just have a run to the latrine, okay?"

"Go. I've got you covered."

Hanson high-tailed to the roadside brush. O'Hara stood waiting, three flatbeds in the line-up, ready to check in. Behind them was Lenny's milk truck.

After each vehicle humped its way to the gate, the driver handed a badge to O'Hara. He examined each carefully, matching face and photo.

"Okay, you're clear," he said to the cigar-chomper manning flatbed number three.

Lenny eased to the gate. O'Hara recited the company mantra.

"ID badge." Lenny handed his over. O'Hara scrutinized it. "What about him," he said, annoyed by the snoring passenger whose face was covered with a copy of the *Battle Hymn Hearth*.

"Kid," Lenny urged, "Where's your ID?"

Ron pulled his badge from his shirt pocket, passed it to Lenny who passed it to O'Hara.

"Kelly!" O'Hara shouted, sending the paper from Ron's face. "Pull over to the shoulder," he commanded.

O'Hara instructed Lenny to stay with the vehicle. On the passenger side, he opened the door. "Please step out of the truck."

Ron obeyed, his shoulders tense, his fists clenched. O'Hara steered him to the back of the van, the noisy refrigeration unit providing cover.

"What are you doing in the milk wagon?"

"Catching a ride to work."

"Why are you coming in the back door and not the main gate?"

"This is closer to where Katherine and me are living."

O'Hara pushed the cap from his forehead.

"I don't get it. I thought you were living with darkies in the old part of town."

"We had to leave," Ron said. "It wasn't safe. Especially after what happened to Isaac Toony."

"Where are you kids calling home?"

Ron pointed down the road. "The Cloverleaf."

"You mean that, that old, you know, the place where…"

"Whorehouse?" Ron said. "It's a diner and a motel that's been fixed up. It's clean and it's safe. The owner's a nice guy named Joe Geary."

O'Hara exposed his palms. "Look, Ron. I'm sorry about everything, about all the trouble you've had," he said. "We want to help, me and Mrs. O'Hara. We want to be involved with you, Katherine and our grandchild."

"Then you know she's pregnant?" Ron said.

"Yes. And I know she wanted to tell me herself, but her mother couldn't keep the secret."

O'Hara moved within arm's reach, offering his hand in friendship.

"Let's start over," he pleaded. "Let's give this a chance."

Ron withdrew.

"That's all Katherine and me ever wanted, a chance, but nobody listened because I'm Protestant and she's Catholic. Christ Almighty, hasn't religion ruined enough lives? What about love? You know, that thing between two people who need each other?"

O'Hara flinched. "Don't take the Lord's name in vain, son. We know you love each other and that's what matters." O'Hara's hand was freefalling but Ron caught it.

"You know, Mr. O'Hara, when I graduate electrician school, I'll get a proper place," he said. "It'll be far away from this ugliness, but close enough to work at the mill."

Lenny leaned on the horn and poked his head out the window.

"Hey. I've gotta get this stuff to the commissary before it turns to cheese."

"Hold your horses, mister, we're almost done here," O'Hara yelled. He took hold of Ron's arm. "What's your room number, son?"

"We're in cabin six, around the back."

Lenny gave the horn another blast.

"You best be on your way, Ron," O'Hara said, turning to leave.

"Wait," Ron said. "I'm sorry if I sounded hard-nosed. Thanks for giving me a chance."

"Get yourself in that truck, son. You'd better study, study, study. You'll have a family to support soon enough."

22.

Ben and Martha felt like they had been on the road for weeks, but in reality the journey from Battle Hymn to Birmingham lasted two grueling days. Finally, one radiator hose, two tires and a muffler later, the DeSoto hiccupped into the Gaston Motel parking lot on a steamy morning.

"We're finally here. Wait in the car, honey. I'll be right back."

Martha, too road-worn to care, would have nodded yes to *honey, jump off the bridge.*

While Ben was gone, her eyes unglazed to discover trim landscape and modern architectural design, all part of a motel built by blacks exclusively for blacks. Ten minutes later, Ben trotted to the car. "I got us a room." He flashed the key.

Martha trudged empty-handed to a ground-floor room. Ben followed, two suitcases in hand. Once inside, they drew the floral print drapes, undressed, collapsed in bed and snored.

A few hours later, mumbling and hurried footsteps sounded in the parking lot. Ben and Martha snored away. The clamor outside reached party level followed by arguing, which woke the couple.

"There will be no violence," one man shouted.

The Toonys stared out the window across the parking lot to the second-story balcony. Men dressed in everything from sharkskin suits to box-cut shirts and field clothes gathered outside Room #30. The group parted like the Red

Sea as Dr. King came to the railing, his hands gripping the black lacquer metal.

"It's not in the service of our people to be like them," he scowled. "We're here to let the world know we want to live peacefully in a free and just society!" Grumblings followed him as he re-entered the room.

Seeing there were no women in attendance, Martha stayed behind. On the second-story balcony, Ben filtered through strangers, moving toward the room's entrance. As he began to enter, an arm shot across the doorway.

"War room members only." Ben's surprise reflected in the man's mirrored sunglasses. Realizing he would get no closer, he leaned against the doorjamb, watching and listening.

Dr. King sat on the edge of the bed while other men rested against the wall.

"Our aim is to shut down business in the downtown area," King said. "The Negro has sufficient buying power. If we withdraw that element, it'll mean the difference between profit and loss for most of those businesses." Heads nodded.

One man, sweat rolling off his chin and into the humid air, stepped forward.

"How do we make sure our people aren't shopping in segregated stores," he asked.

"Good question." The response came from a man sitting in a wooden chair next to Dr. King.

"Well, Ralph, do you have an answer," King asked.

Ralph Abernathy stood, his chin resting in his palm as he paced. After a few seconds of deliberation, he returned to his seat.

"We'll have to do surveillance of our people," he sadly admitted. "And if we find them doing business in those stores, we'll have to shame them into not doing so. After all, we're going to jail for them as well."

Jail? Ben thought. I've never done time.

Another man came to the balcony and reminded everyone, "Be at the16th Street Baptist Church at eight a.m." The group dispersed. As the door shut, Ben's eyes met Dr. King's, exchanging a silent, *Hello, brother.*

Ben returned to find Martha watching a local news report that featured someone identified as Birmingham's Public Safety Commissioner. "Those people know their place," the man said. "If they think some outta town pond scum is gonna disrupt our ways, well, bring 'em on."

Ben switched off the television.

"What went on up there," she asked, unpacking and filling the dresser with their clothes. Ben sat at a round table meant to give a kitchen-feel to the front of the room.

"I saw Dr. King," he said.

"What was he like?" Martha sounded girlish.

"He was busy," Ben replied and flipped through the motel directory.

"There were a lot of men," she said. What's going on?"

"I need a drink."

"Benjamin Toony, when was the last time you took to spirits?"

"Come and sit." He used his foot to shove the other chair from under the table.

"What is it, sweetheart? What did those men say to you?"

"Looks like I'm going to jail."

"Jail? What on earth for?"

"I'm not sure, but everyone who protests tomorrow is going to jail."

Martha jumped to her feet. "Let's get out of here. This isn't what we planned on."

"Honey, please sit."

Martha complied. "You know how these white lawmen treat our people," she said. "You want to end up shot, carved up or dangling from a tree?"

"I'm not going off into the woods. We'll be in broad daylight. There'll be many people and cameras. Besides, those types of barbarians are like cockroaches. They don't do their work in the light of day. They prefer night time and sheets over their faces."

"But jail? What if they do something to you? What if you just up and vanish into thin air. What then?"

"We're here for Isaac, right?" He reached across the table to touch her hands.

She began to sob, "Isaac, my dear Isaac. Our baby boy." Her shoulders shook and Ben kissed her wrist.

"Isaac is what this is all about," he said, absorbing her jolts. "Our boy may not have known it, but he was one of the first soldiers in this new war. Birmingham's where we Toonys draw the line."

He came to her side. She turned and planted her face in his mid-section. "If something happens to you, I'm done for," she cried.

"Nothing's going to happen, honey." His eyes closed. "I'll tell you what. How 'bout we forget everything for a few hours. You get dressed and we'll go to the fancy lounge this place has. I saw a picture of Louis Armstrong on the billboard when I registered. Maybe he's playin' tonight."

* * *

The lounge at the Gaston was first-rate. The greatest black talents in the world graced its stage, but not that night. People ate quiet suppers. They chatted among themselves about the morning march into downtown Birmingham and the danger that might lie ahead. Ben and Martha were seated in an alcove, which provided a view of the entire dining room. They watched as customers came and went, Martha on the lookout for Dr. King.

The lights were low, but from the corner of his eye, Ben noticed a gentleman with cotton-white hair staring in his direction. With him was a handsome woman who looked vaguely familiar.

The waiter, dressed in a red waist-cut jacket, starched white shirt, complete with bowtie, tight black trousers and shoes shined to military spec, came to the table.

"May I offer either of you a cocktail," he inquired, his voice rich with southern hospitality.

Martha eyeballed Ben.

"I'll have club soda with lime."

"Very good, sir. And for madam?"

"A Coke for me, please."

"Of course," the waiter acknowledged. "I'll return shortly with your drinks and take your dinner orders."

After the waiter left, they perused the menu.

"This place is pricy," he said.

"Then don't order pricy stuff," she quipped.

Ben decided on ground sirloin and potato. He closed his menu to find the cotton-topped gentleman still staring.

"Do you know that couple seated over there?" he whispered, his eyes cast to the far end of the dining room.

"Where?"

"Over there," nudging his head.

"Don't stare."

"He's the one who's gawking."

"I need my glasses, I can't see at this distance," she said.

Martha adjusted her eyewear and pretended to examine the menu.

"Don't you know who they are," she asked.

"It's hard to tell."

She took him by the hand.

"Come on. Let's say hello."

They waded through the busy dining room. As they
drew nearer to the other couple, Ben gasped. "Well, I'll be.
It's Tom and Carol Davis!" They went to the Davis table
where the four friends shared a bittersweet reunion.

"Eighteen years, eighteen years," Tom declared,
standing to hold Martha's white-gloved hand.

"Thomas, you always were the gentleman," Martha
whispered, color coming to her face.

Ben and Tom clasped each other's forearms. "My old
friend," Ben said.

"Hey, watch it," Tom guffawed. "I ain't much older than
you."

"Thomas, this is the Gaston, not the Thunderbird," Carol
scolded. "Settle down. You're drawing attention."

"Well, I guess y'all eatin' here, right," Tom asked.

"We got us a table in the corner," Ben replied.

"Nonsense. Y'all eatin' with us."

The Toonys scooted into the banquette. Without notice,
a waiter delivered their Coke and club soda with lime.

"This place is on its toes," Ben pointed out.

"Nothing's better than the Gaston," Carol said.

"Birmingham?" Tom said. "What brings you south?"

"Isaac…" Martha began then bit her lip.

Tom and Carol, puzzled, looked to Martha then Ben.

"Who's he," Tom asked.

Ben's tone grew sullen. "He's our boy."

"Is he comin' here, too?"

"No."

As he explained Isaac's death, all four heads bowed, all
four heads recalling different pasts. Tom cleared his throat,
folded and unfolded his red linen napkin.

"I was about your age when the Lord took Gerald," he said.

Ben's head snapped level. "It wasn't God. It was the devil...the same devil who stole my son."

"You mean that white kid who killed Gerald is still on the loose? He's gotta be a man by now. Are sure it was him?"

"Yes!" Martha's sudden declaration stunned her dinner companions.

"Keep your voice down," Ben whispered.

"I'm, I'm sorry. I can't help it."

Two waiters followed by busboys eased the tension.

After dinner was served, the waiter's supporting cast returned to the kitchen. He reminded his customers, "I'm just a finger snap away."

Carol lifted the lid and inhaled. "I told you. Nothing beats the Gaston."

The rhythm of eating deadened the shock of Martha's earlier statement.

Midway through the meal, Carol broke the silence. "I bet you don't have a place like this up north."

"We don't. Never did," Ben said.

"Ya wanna know why?" Tom said. "I figured it out after I'd been here a few years. Here's how I see it." He wiped his mouth and put down his silverware. "It started after the Civil War. Up North our people always felt accepted. Kind of protected from the no-good cracker by well- intentioned whites. Up there we didn't need to build our own world. The white folks abandoned their run-down neighborhoods and passed them on to us. They called them ghetto or slum. And being thankful niggers, what'd we do? Hell. We moved right in and called them home."

"I wish you wouldn't talk like that," Carol said.

"I'm tellin the truth."

"Well, you can be more polite."

"Anyway, like I was sayin'. They gave us everything they thought we needed and we said 'thank you, sir'." He smiled. "We figured they knew best."

Martha fidgeted while Ben took in every word.

"Down here, black man's a tool, but still an outcast. Cracker doesn't mind us diggin' the ditch, cleanin', cookin' or changin' babies diapers. No sir. That's just fine. But you try and get yourself something in his world? Forget it. You're dead. Let me tell you though, things are changin'. We had to build our own world and we've learned to do it our way. This fine motel and restaurant is what happens when we do things for ourselves. When we dream and we fulfill it. I suspect that's why Dr. King's here. He's got some dream he's workin' on."

After dessert, Tom appeared restless, shifting from side to side as he rubbed his left arm.

"Thomas, are you all right?" Carol said.

"Yeah. I'm fine. Just thinkin' 'bout Gerald."

"Tom, are you marching tomorrow," Ben asked.

"Nah, I'm useless. My feet swell. Carol does the heavy liftin'."

"Women are marching," Martha asked.

"Sure they are," Tom replied. "Woman's just as strong as a man."

"But what if you go to jail, Carol?"

"They can't lock me up no tighter than I've been for the past eighteen years."

Not much else was said after that. Ben didn't even ask where Tom and Carol lived or how they made money. He only knew that he was about to risk everything to honor his son.

23.

The noon whistle thrust the Cloverleaf into high gear. With every seat occupied by sweaty drivers, lunches flew off the grill. After loosening their belts, satiated men made room for the next customers, and paid their bill. Crowding the pickup window, waitresses squabbled and stuck orders to the pinwheel. Geary snatched them, shouting demands to the line cook and the sandwich man. Between ringing up customers, Katherine pitched in. She delivered menus, poured water, and wiped the lunch counter of stray food, ogled by the merry-go-round of roughnecks seated in the booths.

Outside, truckers gathered around the entrance, waiting their chance to eat home cooking. O'Hara's arrival didn't go without notice. He squeezed his squad car between two flatbeds loaded with iron girders. He got out and approached the hungry group. They dispersed.

He looked through the picture window, entered the diner and stood at the end of a line of customers waiting to pay. One by one, they peeled off until O'Hara was next in line.

* * *

"Your check, please," Katherine said. She concentrated on her cash drawer as she cracked a fresh roll of quarters. She extended her hand, waiting for the guest check. Two warm hands took hold of hers.

"Excuse me, but...Daddy! Oh, Daddy!"

She came from behind the register, almost floating into her father's arms.

"My little girl." He took her in his embrace. After the longest minute, he eased her to arms length. "A mother, you, a mother. I can't believe it." Never a hint of anger, his hand touched her stomach. Tenderness filled his eyes.

Katherine wanted to cry.

I'm sorry, Daddy. I had no choice.

Geary took notice of the exchange and came from the kitchen.

"Is there something I can help you with, officer," he asked, standing at Katherine's side.

"Daddy, this is Mr. Geary, the owner."

"Pleased to meet you, Geary. I've heard nice things about you and your place. Are you new in town?"

"Thanks. Yeah. I'm fresh from the Marine Corps. Twenty years."

"Any wife or kids?"

"Nah. Not in the cards for me," Geary said.

Katherine interrupted. "How did you know to come here, Father?"

"I bumped into Ron. We had a nice talk."

"Nice talk? I thought you hated him."

Geary began to feel like a fly in the confessional. "I'll leave you to your business," he said.

"Nice to meet you," O'Hara offered again.

Customers began to stir, signaling their intent to leave. "Here comes another bunch," Geary said.

Katherine waited as the truckers argued over who owed what. After a debate of "not my damn turn," one trucker paid. Then, with toothpicks stuck between their teeth, the drivers made their way to the street.

The connection between Katherine and her father plunged into silence. She fumbled with a nickel roll, almost spilling forty freshly minted coins to the floor. He sat at the counter and observed the Cloverleaf's clientele, which prompted him to ask, "How would you like to come home, Katherine?"

Home to my own bed? Things the way they were. But what if that monster thinks I've told what he did to me?

Deadpan, she said, "And what about Ron? Should I abandon him?"

"Abandon is the wrong word," he said. "I just think you'd be safer with us until Ron gets a proper place to live."

"What makes a place proper," she asked. "Is it a row of houses occupied by people who listen through walls, upset with those that don't share the same likes and dislikes? Or is it beliefs stuffed into heads by a priest on Sunday, who sends them home to hate their neighbors on Monday because religion tells them to?"

O'Hara was caught flatfooted. His daughter spoke rebellion with undeniable clarity.

"Katherine, I know there's hypocrisy," he began, almost apologizing. "It's everywhere in town, but people have to work side-by-side. Most keep their feelings hidden until they're with their own kind. It helps us deal with reality."

"Reality?" She glanced to her stomach then wiped the counter, struggling with a ketchup stain.

Another group of men started toward the register. Geary poked his head from the kitchen. "Honey, take care of these guys."

She stretched and yawned. O'Hara's face turned red when her stomach protruded from the top of her pants.

After the men left, O'Hara looked at his watch. "Think about what I said, will you? I've got to get back to work." She walked him to the door and watched as he drove away. *I wish I could tell you, Daddy.*

* * *

A man hunched on the last stool near the wall, his face performing its own peek-a-boo from behind the front page of the *Hearth* as he observed the interaction between Katherine and O'Hara.

When Katherine returned to the counter, the man put down his paper, finished his coffee and came to the register. She counted money, separating twenties, tens, fives and singles.

"I'll be right with you," she said, concentrated on stuffing the cash into an envelope.

"No problem, sweetie," the man said. "I've got all the time in the world for you."

Deaf to his remark, she took his check without looking, focused on pushing the right buttons. "Let me see," she said. "That'll be $3.75 for coffee, chicken-fried steak, potatoes and a slice of cobbler."

"Ya didn't tell your old man about our cozy little get-together, did ya?"

"It's you," she screamed. Her hand shot up and slapped Bob Kelly's face.

"Who do ya think ya're," he growled. "I'll show ya."

He raised his arm to crack her head. As it swept down with all its fury, another hand swallowed it. He looked over his shoulder, Geary towering over him, a smile on his face.

"Something I can help you with, pal," Geary asked.

Kelly struggled to break free and Katherine rose from a crouching, protect-me position.

"Let go of me or..."

"Or what? You worm." Geary cranked Kelly's arm. "Pay the little lady and you'll be on your way." He twisted until Kelly reached in his pocket and spilled three singles and three quarters. "Don't forget the tip," Geary added, giving an extra jolt.

"Fuck ya, ya bastard."

Geary responded with bone-crunching force until Kelly slid a single across the counter. "I'll get ya," he cursed, glaring at Katherine. "Ya little bitch."

Katherine mouthed, I didn't tell anybody.

Geary gave another twist. "The little what, my friend?" He spun Kelly into a hammerlock and directed him to the front door. By this time, the staff and remaining customers were well into the show and applauded the final act. Geary kicked the door open and applied his foot to Kelly's ass.

"Thanks for stopping by," he said, catapulting Kelly into the parking lot. "Oh, and by the way, don't come back or you'll be leavin' with one arm."

"I'll be back, ya giant asshole," Kelly said, massaging his shoulder. "Ya haven't seen the last of me."

24.

O'Hara thought in circles, trying to figure a way to bring his daughter home. Each time he began he ended up at the same conclusion: she's as stubborn as her mother. The cycle kept on until the security phone buzzed. "Truck Gate," he mumbled.

"O'Hara?" It was Captain Sullivan. "I need you to come by the main building. You can have the outbound guard keep an eye for any inbound traffic."

O'Hara checked the time: Twenty minutes until the whistle. "I'll stop by after the whistle, Captain."

"Nah, nah, get in your squad car and shoot over now."

"On my way, Captain."

Ten minutes later, O'Hara arrived at corporate headquarters. What the hell kind of news does the captain have, he wondered as he walked the shiny corridor and entered the captain's office.

"Ah, there you are, John, take a seat," Sullivan said, all cozied with his feet on the desk, hands folded across his chest.

"No thanks, Captain. I've been on my hams all day."

"Well, I hope you liked it because that's part of what I need to tell you."

"What's that, sir?"

"Do you like good news first or would you rather have the bad?" Sullivan stubbed his cigarette and stood.

"Your choice, sir."

"Number one," Sullivan began, "relax. You makin' me feel like a goddamn commandant."

O'Hara's posture softened.

"That's better. Now, I know you don't like being out in the boonies, but something's come up."

Oh shit! What did I do to piss him off?

Sullivan sat on the edge of his desk. "Do you remember I told you old Shamus was caught sleepin'?"

"Yes, Captain."

"Well, the poor geezer wasn't asleep. He had himself a career ending heart attack. The medical guys say he's done for."

"I'm sorry for him, Captain. Shamus is a good guy."

"You're gonna be takin' his place. There's nobody who can handle that position like you."

O'Hara's chin dropped.

"That's the bad news. The good news is you got yourself the squad car to keep. You can drive it home or to China for all I give a damn. But make sure it's on your own time, Johnny-boy."

Normally, this assignment would have been considered a demotion, but the thought of seeing his daughter on a regular basis brought a faint smile.

"Whatever you need from me, Captain."

Sullivan, now behind the desk, intoned, "You're a good man, always doing the right thing. Why you never made it up the ranks, I'll never know."

Actually, they both knew. All the old-timers knew.

The whistle blasted. "Is there anything else, sir?"

"No. Thanks for taking it like a man."

"Aye, aye, Captain."

O'Hara paused on the front steps of the corporate building.

"Now I can keep an eye on her. Thank you, Jesus," he whispered to the sky.

As he drove, he noticed a man walking backwards, his thumb protruding, his other hand managing a bundle.

O'Hara hit the siren and red lights. *There's no hitching rides on company roads.*

A few yards from the hitcher, the squad car skidded to a halt. O'Hara opened the door, planted one foot on the ground and poked his head over the roof of the car.

"Ron, you idiot," he said. "You wanna get canned? Get your rear end in here before one of those corporate boys sees you."

Ron tossed his books on the front seat and jumped in. O'Hara killed the cop accessories.

"What are you doing hitchin' on the company road?"

"It's the only way back to the Cloverleaf."

The squad car peeled out, spewing loose gravel.

"I saw Katherine today," O'Hara said.

"You went to the diner?"

"I sat at the counter and talked to her. The place looks okay, but I hate her havin' to be around the creeps who eat there," O'Hara admitted.

The car approached the outbound security gate. O'Hara waved to the night guard and continued toward the Cloverleaf.

"I have a proposition, Ron."

"What kind of proposition."

"You got a ride in the morning, right?"

"So far so good."

The squad car came up on a struggling eighteen-wheeler laden with expansion girders. As the truck burped exhaust, climbing through gears, the squad car kept pace.

"It turns out that I'll be workin' the truck entrance for the foreseeable future," O'Hara said.

"And," Ron asked.

"And don't interrupt," O'Hara said. "I have use of the car. I'll bring you back to the diner every day if you persuade Katherine to come home while you're takin' classes."

"We already discussed her going home," Ron said, "but we decided to stick it out together. I'll talk to her about it again. That's the best I can do."

"I asked her," O'Hara said, "but she's as stubborn and hardheaded as her mother. She won't leave you."

Ron's tone sharpened. "Now why did you go and ask her that? I thought you were gonna give us a chance."

"Don't get peeved, boy. I'm just thinkin' of her and the child you're bringin' into the world. I'd have you both come to our house if it wouldn't set off World War III, but you – especially you – you know what the consequences are, mixing in our own back yard."

"I'll ask her," Ron said, his voice deflated. "That's the best I can do."

"Well, if you ask her and she still wants to stay, I'll keep my end of the bargain and bring you back to the diner each night. How's that?"

"It's a fair deal, Mr. O'Hara."

"Then it's a deal," he said.

O'Hara downshifted, punched the gas and sped past the lumbering flatbed. Two miles later, he wheeled to the side of the road, just short of the diner.

"Get out here, Ron. I don't want her to think I prodded you. If she thinks that, she'll never come home."

25.

The bar crowd hung on Duffy's every word: Higgins, Loughery, Finny, but no Bob Kelly.

"Let me tell you," Duffy boasted. "Me and Bob caused a lot of shit in our day. Nobody fucked with us."

"Tell the story, you know the one, about how you guys taught that darkie a lesson when you was kids," Higgins said.

"Not much to tell. The store lit up like a bonfire. It was hot enough to fry chicken."

Tickled by Duffy's humor, the gang of inebriants pounded the bar.

In the parking lot, a '57 Chevy pick-up truck rumbled to a halt. Kelly got out rubbing his arm, opening the bar door with his foot. All eyes scrolled his way.

"Bob, you dumb shit!" Duffy bellowed. "You're one drink down. Get your spud-ass in here. Tommy, set us up all around and make Kelly's a double."

Kelly, still massaging his arm, took up the usual seat on the corner of the bar, directly across from Duffy.

Shots in hand, Duffy toasted, "And here's to Catholics and jiggaboos who stick their nose where it don't belong!"

"Here! Here!" the group cheered. After collective "Ahs," empty shot glasses hit the bar in unison.

"Hey Bob. What's with the arm? You been poundin' your pud too hard," Duffy teased.

"Oh screw ya, scumbag," he shot back. "It just so happens I ran in to my Catholic daughter-in-law today."

"What the fuck you talkin' about," Duffy said.

Loughery, Higgins and Finny leaned forward on their stools, eyes wide, elbow-to-elbow, awaiting Kelly's punch line.

"Yeah, I stopped by the old whorehouse out near the truck entrance for a bite to eat and there she was, running the cash register. That asshole, O'Hara, was there too. They was chattin' it up a bit, but they didn't see me. After her old man left I went to pay the little piece of ass a visit. I thought she might have let O'Hara know how good I gave it to her. But ya know what?" He looked each man in the eye. "The little bitch slapped me. Can ya believe it?"

"You didn't let her get away with that, did you?" Duffy said.

"I went to knock her upside the head, but this giant asshole snuck up on me and twisted my arm then threw me the hell out."

"Was your boy there?"

"Nah. But I'll tell ya what, I'd like to get another shot at the sonofabitch who tossed me out." Kelly's eyes twinkled. "Hey Duffy, what ya say you, me and Loughery take us a little ride tonight?"

"You know me. I never miss a party," Duffy replied.

"How 'bout ya, Loughery? We'll use your truck in case someone remembers me driving there today."

"You're the boss. Whatever you say."

Kelly's arm shot into the air. "Tommy, ya better get us nice 'n' fueled up."

The sun dropped below the horizon and the rust-colored sky turned black. After six more shots, three determined drunks drove out to the far end of the steel mill. Along the way, they stopped to fill empty whiskey bottles with gasoline.

* * *

Ron entered the diner to find Katherine seated in Geary's booth, thumbing through the *Hearth.* There were few customers. Most truckers were in their sleepers nuzzled with girlie magazines or listening to the ballgame on transistors.

"Hey," he said, sliding to her side. "How's the most beautiful girl in the world?"

"Stop, Ron. I'm fat and feel like I've been stuffed into my skin."

"It's only temporary," he replied, touching her belly.

"What are those," she asked, pointing to three books stacked on the tabletop.

"When they said school, they meant it." Ron smirked, "What did I get myself into? It's like high school. I've got homework, tests and everything."

"Huh, huh," she mumbled, concentrated on a newspaper article.

"What did you do today, baby," he asked.

No response.

"Katherine," he whined, "what did you do?"

She raised her head. "Today?" Her voice was innocent and she looked around the room.

"No, tomorrow," he replied.

Geary came to the booth, wiping oily hands on the mast of his apron.

"You two ready for those free dinners?"

"What free…"

Geary cut him off. "Before you order," he said, "let me tell ya what's eighty-six'd."

He grabbed a menu and ran down the list: "No turkey, outta chicken-fried steak, chili's done for. Let's see, that's 'bout it. Whaddya have?"

"Why are we gettin' free dinner," Ron asked.

"Didn't she tell you?" Geary looked at Katherine.

"I'm gonna run the cash register during breakfast and lunch," she confessed.

"Oh. I never planned on you working," Ron waited a beat. "But I guess it's good to save money," he admitted. "What about getting rest? You can't be on your feet all day, can you?"

Katherine slapped the newspaper. "I'm pregnant, not crippled. What do you expect me to do all day? Count knots in the pine paneling?" Then she mindlessly re-thumbed the *Hearth*.

Now a tower of impatience, Geary asked, "Excuse me, kids. I'd like to clean up the kitchen."

"Sorry, Joe, I'll have chicken pot pie," Katherine said.

"Make it two."

"Sounds like a winner," Geary said.

"Is it okay if I crack a window," Ron asked.

"Sure, kid."

With Geary in the kitchen, Ron watched and listened as the day fizzled out. The Cloverleaf's green neon light crept over the diner. The throb of diesel motors competed with crickets, tree frogs and the occasional loon. He took hold of Katherine's hand and spun the wedding band on her finger.

"Do you really want to work here," he asked.

"I might as well," she replied as she skimmed the newspaper.

"You know," he began, unsure of his next words. "I, I was thinking about what you said."

"What did I say?" She flipped to the front page.

"Well, maybe it would be a good idea for you to go home while I get this school stuff out of the way."

She smacked her fists to the table. Geary poked his head through the pick-up window.

She lowered her voice to an angry whisper. "After all that guff about 'we're in it together, let's stick it out, things will be worse on Wood Street,' you changed your mind? Just like that?"

"Not just like that, Katherine." Ron glanced toward the idling trucks and at the few drivers finishing their meals. "This place is a little rough. I'm worried about you being here alone."

"Alone? I'm not alone," she replied, looking toward the kitchen. "I've got the biggest bodyguard in the world."

"We barely know the guy," Ron whispered.

In her head, Katherine replayed the Geary-Kelly incident, but decided not to mention it. "I wouldn't worry about Joe. He's a man you can count on."

"How do you know?"

"I have a gut feeling."

"Okay, if you say so," Ron said, content that he had fulfilled Mr. O'Hara's request.

"I say so," Katherine said then she began reciting the headlines.

"UNRULY GANG OF NEGROES JAILED BY BIRMINGHAM POLICE."

Below the caption were photos depicting recent events that had unfolded in Birmingham, Alabama.

"Look, Ron," she said, yanking his sleeve and pointing to the photo of protesters pinned to store fronts by fire hoses and snarling dogs.

Ron frowned and smeared his face with both hands. "Jesus, that's where the Toonys went."

"Don't say Jesus, Ron. It's a sin."

"That's the goddamn sin," he said, finger jammed to the photo.

He examined the other shots: police clubbing a black man kneeling on the ground, more fire hose assaults and one that was tranquil, almost like a funeral procession. It depicted black people peacefully walking arm-in-arm toward downtown Birmingham. A caption below the shot identified a man in the front as Dr. Martin Luther King, "the ringleader."

Besides Ron and Katherine, there was one other customer. He got up from his chicken-fried steak and switched on the portable TV Geary had placed at the end of the lunch counter. "Oh good," he groaned as he adjusted the rabbit ears, "just in time for the evening news."

Ron and Katherine turned their attention to the newscaster's gravel voice.

"The Reverend Martin Luther King has been released from jail where he spent twenty-four hours in solitary confinement. President Kennedy has sent a strongly worded message to Governor George Wallace denouncing the arrest of peaceful protesters in Birmingham. The president vows an investigation will be conducted. For his part, Dr. King stated that 'no amount of brutality will derail this peaceful protest against violence and the disease of segregation'."

After Dr. King's statement, a film clip of George Wallace's remarks played. He stood on the steps of the Governor's mansion, his voice defiant.

"We'll let no gang of outsiders come into the great state of Alabama and tell us how to run our business. These protesters are rabble-rousers sent here to agitate peaceful Negroes."

Ron studied the photo of marchers. "Katherine," he elbowed her. "Look. There in the second row." His finger rested beneath a man's face.

Katherine hunched closer to the paper. "It's Mr. Toony. Where's Martha?"

"So that's why they went there," Ron said. "I wouldn't worry about Martha. Ben probably had the good sense to keep her out of danger." His hand ran up and down Katherine's back.

"I hope they're okay," she said. There was a trickle of sadness in her voice.

"When they get back I'm gonna stop over there to see how they're doin'," Ron said.

"You'd better not. Remember what Mr. Toony said about us being in his neighborhood?"

"Gees. It's not like I'm not going tonight. I'll wait a while."

Geary brought the steaming potpies to the table. "Here you go guys. Enjoy." He went to the TV and lowered the sound. The lone trucker frowned. Geary smiled. The trucker deposited exact change on the counter, grunted "Good food," and left.

An hour later, Ron, Katherine and Geary stood outside at the base of the sign. Geary flicked the switch. If the trio had not been blinded by sudden darkness, they might have noticed the outline of a pick-up truck parked a half-mile down the road.

"I'm exhausted," Geary sighed. "I've gotta hit the rack."

"I've gotta study," Ron said.

"I'll read the rest of the newspaper," Katherine added as they strolled to the cabins.

"Goodnight," Geary yawned as he entered cabin number one.

Ron and Katherine waved and went to cabin number six. The other cabins were empty. After a few minutes, Geary's room went dark. Ron and Katherine's room remained bright.

* * *

"Do ya remember this place?" Kelly joked. "When we were kids we used to get more ass than a toilet seat here." He toked his Lucky and passed a pint of booze to Duffy.

"Looky there," Duffy said as he brought the bottle to his lips. He pointed toward the diner.

"It's the giant asshole," Kelly cursed.

"Is that the guy who wrung your arm," Loughery asked.

"That's the fucker," Kelly said, his eyes squinted. He strained to see who was with Geary. "Jackpot!" he whispered. "We've got ourselves a real trifecta."

"What jackpot?" Duffy said.

"It's the lovely Katherine O'Hara and my traitor son. Looks like we'll be baggin' three birds tonight."

"You're not thinkin' of blastin' your own boy, are you?" Duffy asked as drool seeped down the corners of his mouth.

Kelly snatched the bottle and pulled a deep swig. "He's no kin of mine. Not after marryin' her."

"I guess you're right," Duffy admitted, scratching the top of his head. "He shoulda known better."

"I taught him the way to live," Kelly continued, "but his mother kept interferin'. Now it's payback time."

Their heads nodded in unison as the Cloverleaf sign was extinguished. They puffed cigarettes and strained to see who went to what cabin.

"There's one light out." Kelly let loose a belch from hell. "We'll wait for the other one. Snuff the butts and get ready to uncork those bottles."

Loughery and Duffy fumbled and complied. Kelly handed each an oil rag.

"Okay, fellas," he slurred. "Put these in ya pocket. When we get out of the truck, stuff 'em in the bottlenecks. Make sure they're damn tight. Ya don't want gas leakin' on ya when you toss those babies through the window."

* * *

Ron fell asleep on the last page of the first chapter: WIRE CODE AND COLOR. Katherine, in nothing but panties, sprawled on the foldout bed. She considered telling him about his father coming to the diner, but the way Geary had handled the situation allowed her put the thought out of her mind. *Why cause trouble.* Instead, she studied photos of the Birmingham protest.

"Ron, who do you believe?"

He stirred and replied, "Believe?" His face was pressed to the pages of the textbook. "I believe there's a lot I don't know."

Katherine flipped to her back, her belly a small mound of Jell-O. "I mean about the protesters, you idiot. Do you think the Negroes are to blame or that Governor Wallace?"

Ron peeled his face from the pages, rubbing sleep from his eyes. "I can't imagine Ben and Martha taking part in a violent act. It's as absurd as my father helping old ladies cross the street."

"Why'd you bring him up," Katherine said.

"I dunno. Just conversation, I guess."

He scrambled to change the subject. "Hey. Do you want to hear something dumb?"

"Not really," she replied, sliding under the covers.

"Oh, come on now. Be a sport."

"Okay. What is it?"

He flipped a few pages of the textbook. "Here," he said. "Listen to this. The proper wiring of multiple circuits requires matching pole to pole. To ensure safety and accuracy, a universal wiring color code was developed."

Katherine rolled to her side. "That's it? It sounds boring, but what's dumb about it?"

"No. No. That's just the set-up. You see, there are ten colors of wire and they're deployed in the same order by all electricians."

"How do they remember the order?"

"Well, they've constructed a little nursery rhyme. That's the dumb thing."

"Read it to me."

"Let me tell you the order of the wire colors first."

"Okay." Katherine showed some interest.

"Here goes. Brown, Black, Red, Orange, Yellow, Green, Blue, Violet, Gray and White."

"That is a lot to remember, Ron."

"Yeah, but listen to the rhyme. Bad Boys Rape Our Young Girls But Violet Gives Willingly."

Katherine's jaw clenched. Finally, her eyes welled then she buried her face in the pillow.

Ron came to her side. "It's only a stupid rhyme," he said, trying to soothe her.

She rolled to face him. "It's sick is what it is! How could anybody joke about that?"

"You're right," He kissed her forehead. "I'm sorry. I'll never refer to it again."

He undressed, doused the light and hopped into bed. Before too long, they were both fast asleep.

* * *

Loughery and Duffy snored between bouts of not breathing. Kelly had planted his palms on the dashboard, a lion waiting to pounce. But as whiskey was winning, he saw only blurs. Covering one eye improved his vision.

"Oh! Oh!" he whispered. "There we go. Both lights are out. It's dark as a coon's ass." He looked to his right. Duffy's head rested on Loughery's shoulder.

"Oh, Mr. and Mrs. Asshole?" Kelly nudged Duffy's shoulder.

"Not now, sweetie," Duffy mumbled.

"Hey! Wake the fuck up," Kelly said, short of screaming.

The two stirred. Loughery farted and Duffy searched for a cigarette.

"Fuck the cigarette," Kelly said. "There'll be plenty of smoke soon enough."

He rubbed his blubbery face and smacked his lips. "Now listen carefully, Loughery. I need you to do just as I say."

Loughery examined his gums in the rear-view mirror.

"Hey, ya dumb ass! This ain't no foolin' around," Kelly barked.

"Okay, Bob, I'm...I'm with ya. Want do you want me to do?"

"Start the engine, but no revving. Ya gotta build speed without shiftin'."

One hundred yards before reaching the cabins, following Kelly's instruction, Loughery cut the engine and coasted to a quiet stop.

"Take your cue from me, boys," Kelly said. "When I light my rag ya do the same. When they're cookin', we throw 'em and hightail it the fuck outta here."

"Ga...ga...got ya, Boss," Loughery stammered.

"It's just like old days," Duffy replied, now chipper and ready for business.

Loughery pulled on the door handle. Duffy, seated in the middle, waited. Kelly siphoned the last drops of whiskey from a pint and grabbed the sack containing bottles of gasoline. Loughery opened the door and came face-to-face with a Colt .45, its cold barrel pressed to his cheek.

"Evening, boys. Nice night, isn't it?" Geary's Cheshire smile exposed his crooked teeth. He kneed the truck door closed. In his left hand he held a small flashlight, which scanned his surprised guests. "I thought I told you to never show your puss around here," he said, eyes fixed on Kelly and shoving the gun deeper into Loughery's face.

Kelly made a quick move. Geary cocked the hammer.

"What ya goin' for, chubby?" The light hit Kelly's liquor-logged eyes.

Slowly, Geary directed the light to the floorboard, all while denting Loughery's jaw with cold steel.

"You shouldn't have," Geary said, focused on the sack and three bottles at Kelly's feet. "I'm not a drinkin' man."

Kelly smelled an opportunity. "It ain't no booze. It's just some gas. Ya see?" He held one of the bottles directly in the beam. "We're just bringin' it to our buddy. That's all. He called and said his pickup truck ran out of gas."

Geary waited a beat. "I don't see anybody here. Do you?"

"Nah," replied Kelly.

"Okay, then," Geary said. "You best be on your way, but before you leave…" He held out his hand. "The sack and the gas, if you please. I'll just keep it here in case your friend with the empty tank comes driving up."

Kelly passed the bag to Loughery who passed it out the window. Geary smiled as he took the sack. He relaxed the pressure on Loughery's face and slowly stepped away from the truck, never lowering his weapon. "Nice, isn't it?" he said, rolling his head toward the pistol. "It was a gift from the United States Marine Corps."

Using the barrel, he directed Loughery to start the engine. "Now, this is the last time for all of you," he said. "Don't come back or you'll make me do something you'll regret. Get the fuck out!"

Loughery fired up the truck. It inched like a punished dog to the road. Geary stood watch until the taillights disappeared and he remained on guard for most of the night.

26.

Dr. White, a kindly, tall man, delivered most of Wood Street's babies – Catholic and Protestant. Being the steel mill's company physician, matters of the soul were checked curbside before entering his downtown office.

After waiting five minutes, Katherine entered a small room, donned a gown and lay on an exam table as the doctor skimmed her abdomen with a stethoscope and checked the vitals. Afterward, he lit an Old Gold cigarette, absorbed a lungful of smoke and snuffed the butt in a nearby ashtray.

"One drag," he said, his voice husky with phlegm. "That's all I allow myself nowadays."

"Are you done, Doc," she asked.

"All done. You don't smoke, do you?"

"Never."

"Good. I read studies that say those things aren't good for you."

Katherine avoided the smell of smoke. She breathed through her mouth, and got dressed while the doctor made notes in her file.

"You're coming along nicely," he said, hanging his clipboard on a wall hook. "Everything looks and sounds normal. You should be delivering right on time."

Delivering right on time? Oh God, help me.

After the exam, she waved down a cab on the main drag. "Where to," the cabby asked.

"Saint Ann's," she said. "And don't go by way of Wood Street."

"Fine with me, kid."

The ride took an extra five minutes, but the cab pulled in front of the church steps at 9:00, just in time for morning mass. She opened her change purse. The cab's meter read $2.50.

"All I have is a five dollar bill. Do you have change?"

"You're my first fare. Don't you have anything else?"

Her shoulders drooped. "No. This is it, but I'll need a ride home when mass is over."

"Where's home?"

"The Cloverleaf."

"You mean that joint out in the boondocks?"

"Yes. That's where I'm staying – temporarily."

The driver eyeballed her stomach. "How long you gonna be in church?"

"Thirty minutes. Mass is shorter on weekdays."

The cabby slouched in his seat and pulled his cap over his brow. "I'll wait here 'til you're done," he said. "Five bucks should cover the round-trip."

Katherine scurried up the steps and into the church vestibule. She clipped a white hanky to her hair and dipped her finger in holy water then blessed herself. She went directly to the pew her family had occupied each Sunday for the past twenty years. Father Ryan, draped in green and gold vestments, came onto the altar from a side entrance. With him were two altar boys. Their grins of, "Yeah, we get out of class for this," were wiped clean when the priest turned and bowed to a large crucifix one of the boys carried.

There were only a handful of worshipers that morning. Most were old folks wanting to keep their souls spotless as their days on earth ticked off the calendar. Others of varying age appeared sad or overcome by guilt. Katherine, one of the latter, craved that which would empower her to start all over again – forgiveness.

Father Ryan faced his flock. He blessed them and recited, "In nomine Patris, et Filii, et Spiritus Sancti."

Those who could stand got to their feet. But all mumbled, "Amen."

Katherine didn't understand Latin nor did most of Saint Ann's Parishioners. She used a translation card to follow along.

Father Ryan continued, "Dominus vobiscum."

Some of the congregation responded, "Et cum spiritu tuo." Katherine answered in English, "And may the Lord also be with you."

Father Ryan followed with, "Fratres, agnoscamus peccata nostra, ut apti simus ad sacra mysteria celebranda."

She pressed her palms to her eyes, reliving the sin that had drawn her to search for absolution. Next, she murmured the Penitential Rite: "I confess to almighty God, and to you, my brothers and sisters that I have sinned through my own fault." She struck her breast and continued. "In my thoughts and in my words, in what I have done and in what I have failed to do; and I ask blessed Mary ever virgin, all the Angels and Saints, and you, my brothers and sisters, to pray for me to the Lord our God."

Father Ryan began the Mass as if it were his last, each word weighted with piety.

The solemn pace intensified Katherine's sense of guilt. She could barely wait to receive communion. Fifteen minutes later, after the Lord's Prayer, the Sign of Peace, and Agnus Dei, the priest raised a wafer of unleavened bread over a gold chalice. He recited in Latin as Katherine murmured in English, "This is the Lamb of God Who takes away the sins of the world. Happy are those who are called to His supper. Lord I am not worthy to receive You, but only say the word and I shall be healed."

After the prayer, one of the altar boys used a felt-tipped mallet to strike a bell, which produced a mournful gong. People wanting communion rose and walked to the railing that separated the altar from the rest of the world. Those who could kneel did while others stood. Katherine knelt at the altar, midway in the group of twelve. She looked to her left, following Father Ryan as he moved down the line. An altar boy, who held a gold plate under the mouth of each person just in case a particle of the host should fall, shadowed him. The priest paused in front of the penitents, their heads tilted back and eyes closed like baby birds about to be fed. Before placing the wafer on the their outstretched tongue he recited, "Corpus Christi." The person responded, "Amen." The priest followed with, "Sanguis Christi." The response: "Amen."

When he reached the man to her left, Katherine, knowing she was next, closed her eyes and stuck out her tongue. She heard the man next to her whisper the second "Amen" and her heart rose, for salvation was at hand. She felt the breeze of Father Ryan's vestments as his shadow darkened the inside of her eyelids. Her tongue ached, but her spirit soared. She felt a second stirring of air. She peeked and saw Father Ryan standing in front of the person to her right and reciting, "Corpus Christi."

Nausea swept through her. It appeared as though there were some sins God and Father Ryan would not forgive. She braced her arm on the railing and pushed herself to standing. Her knees wobbled, both hands clutching at her heart as if to prevent it from exploding in her chest. Turning, she faced the congregation only to feel cold stares, for never had a soul been refused communion at Saint Ann's. At first she took tiny steps, not sure if her legs would give way. Once in the aisle she looked to the exit, which appeared to be miles in the distance. With her soul crushed, her hands supporting her pregnant belly and tears streaming down her cheeks, she moved toward the door, all eyes except those of Father Ryan escorting her.

Outside and alone, she moved step-by-step to the waiting cab. She got in and screamed, "Take me to hell."

27.

Ben and Martha returned to Battle Hymn two weeks after experiencing the power of non-violent protest in Birmingham. Though he had run the gauntlet of arrest, billy club and jail, Ben vowed to bring the fight for peaceful integration home.

For some men, it was the VFW; for others, the Union Hall or local tavern served as a place to congregate. But not all men had been in the armed forces nor were all men members of a union and some men did not drink. Nonetheless, they all, at one time or another, needed haircuts. Archie's Barbershop was the only game in town, if you were white. Blacks were relegated to living room or back porch clippings at the hands of friends or family. When Ben's hair began to spring, he walked to the main drag and paid Archie a visit.

He entered the establishment like a man who felt at home, but strange scents of Old Spice, Aqua Velva, Vitalis and Brylcreem laced with cigar smoke choked his eyes and nose. Barbers manning the six chairs snipped away as if trimming a hedge. When they saw a middle aged black man in the entryway, all work ceased. The heads of waiting customers peered over the top of copies of the *Hearth*. Archie, a squat man with bullfrog features, met Ben just inside the door.

"What can I do for you, boy," he asked.

"Do I look like a boy to you, sir," Ben said.

"Let's not get technical. What do you want? Shine some shoes?"

"I don't shine shoes. I'm…"

"You don't have to tell me who you are. What're you here for?"

"I need a haircut."

"A what?" Archie almost swallowed the cigar stub stuck between his lips. He swung his head around to address the onlookers. "Charlie, you hear that?"

"I'm not sure, but did he ask for a haircut?"

"Yeah. That's what the boy said."

Ben eyes watered with anger. He tightened his fists and his jaw. He made a move to get past Archie's globed-shaped body and into the waiting area.

"Hold it now. You know better than to come here. We don't do nappy hair."

"You don't have to do it," Ben said. "Just shave it. That doesn't require skill."

"You don't get it, boy. We don't touch you darkies! Now git before something happens."

"Something's gonna happen," Ben warned as he strode to the door.

"Now come on, son. We don't want any trouble." Archie went to the door and rested his arm on Ben's shoulder. "You don't mean what you say, do you? Be a good boy and go on home and we'll forget all about this. Okay?"

After wiping Archie's hand from his shoulder, Ben exited the shop.

That evening, Ben felt a new sense of purpose. He was selling ideas. His first move: organize a boycott. Friends and neighbors attended a meeting he had put together. Martha set up several card tables in the hardware store and prepared refreshments. The first jingle came at 6:30. After that, the doorbell jingled until the store was standing room only. Ben came from behind the denim curtain. He carried a hand-painted sign and pinned it to the wall, after which he stood back and murmured the words,

BATTLE HYMN, PENNSYLVAINA
NAACP
EQUAL RIGHTS FOR ALL

"Who's for equality," he asked, turning to the group.

"We are!" came the boisterous response.

He raised his arms above his head. "There's only one way out of *this* Battle Hymn," his voice not unlike Dr. King's. "We must organize and use all peaceful means to let our white brothers know that the days of 'boy' and 'yaz sur' are gone forever."

The group applauded and cheered.

"We can no longer stand by and watch our brothers and sisters be shoved to the back of the line."

There were bursts of, "Here, here. Tell it, brother!"

Ben wiped his brow with a white hanky. He was in awe of his performance for he had never spoken in public. The group was in the palm of his hand and he liked it.

"The time has come," he continued, "to demand equal pay, equal treatment in the workplace, respect for our children, and to be able to walk the streets of Battle Hymn with our heads held high, with pride for our African heritage, for we too are American men and women!"

Applause erupted and feet stomped the old floorboards. Martha offered him a glass of water and rubbed his arm.

"Ben, be careful," she whispered in his ear. "These folks have a lot of pent-up anger. We don't want a riot on our hands."

Ben jerked in surprise. "A riot?" he mouthed, looking toward the jeering crowd, many who were sheepish neighbors, but now their eyes screamed for vengeance.

"You're right, Martha. I'll tone it down."

He sipped some water. "People, people," he shouted and the group calmed. "This is not a call to act out in frustration. If we give in to our weakness and lash out, we'll play right into the hands of those who would cheer our failure. We must be peaceful and incite no one to violence. That was the first thing Dr. King taught me."

"What are we going to do, write nasty letters," one man asked. The crowd snickered.

Ben pointed to the sign pinned on the wall. "NAACP. Do you know what that means?" he said.

No response.

"It stands for the National Association for the Advancement of Colored People. Please take note of the word 'Advancement'."

He waded into the group, moving from table to table, glad-handing people in the aisle. "Yes, advancement," he continued, stopping where a mother held a child in her lap. "May I," he asked, his arms outstretched. The mother passed the little girl to Ben. He cradled her as if she were his as he continued the foray into the audience. The crowd hushed enough to hear its collective breathing.

"Most of you knew my boy, Isaac. He never got the chance to live a full life, but this little girl," Ben almost whispered, "she's our future. She is the one who will benefit from what we build here tonight. She will tell your grandchildren of how you restrained your anger and refused to fall into the trap of violence. She will hold her head high and so will her children and their children." He returned the baby to her mother's arms. "Yes, it is time to act, but act peacefully. It's time to open the door to this child's future," he said.

"What are we going to do," a woman shouted.

Ben moved behind the counter. "We have to target a business downtown. And by target I don't mean with a gun." Some of the group laughed. "We have to select a business that doesn't treat us as equals."

"Who do you have in mind, the whole town," the woman with the baby inquired.

"Well, Archie's Barbershop seems obvious."

Nods and grunts followed.

"What we gonna do," someone yelled. "All ask for a haircut?"

"No," Ben said. "I already did that and Archie sent me packing."

Ben moved to the sign. "Equal Rights for All," he said. "I want thirty volunteers to picket that barbershop. We'll carry signs identifying us as the Battle Hymn chapter of the NAACP. Equal Rights for All will be painted prominently on each of our placards. We'll march in front of that place until we wear a hole in the sidewalk or Archie hires a black barber."

Again, the group showered its approval, stomping the floor, hooting and whistling. The response traveled beyond the walls of the store, loud enough for two men who stood in the shadows across the street to hear.

"When's it happening, Ben," one man blurted. "Yeah," another hollered, "when?"

"Now hold your horses!" Ben's voice grew raspy and faint, unlike Dr. King's.

"We..." he coughed and pinched his Adam's apple. Martha offered him more water and a smile. "We need to do this thing proper. Our civil rights are being pushed to the front burner in the news and on TV." He gulped from his glass. "Now is the time to plan and later is the time to execute."

Ben thought in disbelief, *Am I saying this stuff?*

"I have word that Dr. King is planning to march on Washington, D.C., next month. A week prior to his march, the newspapers will be covering his every move. That's when we plan our demonstration," he said, wiping his brow again.

He produced a yellow sheet of paper. "Come sign up," he demanded, his finger jamming the countertop. "It's now or never!"

28.

In a moment of weakness Katherine said, "I needed help so I went to church and that priest sent me away." Ron paid little attention, his head wrapped around electrical codes and wiring schematics.

"Are you even listening to me?" she said.

"Yeah, every word." He flipped the page of his bible-thick textbook.

"I'm never going to church again. To hell with God."

He said nothing.

"And I'm done with praying. It's for fools." She waited for the big speech, for if she were still at home it would be just about this time that her father would crank up the rhetoric about how speaking ill of God would condemn her soul.

Ron studied away and mumbled, "That's nice. I could go for a dip in a pool."

She wanted to scream, but she didn't.

* * *

As August baked the city, Katherine grew darker. She sat alone in the cabin or sulked in the diner. However, this was not the case for the rest of the town. The steel mill's production cycle had begun. And dominated by the cold hard truth of steel, Battle Hymn geared up for a new season of soot and rumbling trucks. Geary welcomed the resurrection as the Cloverleaf came back to life.

* * *

A series of loud knocks woke Katherine. She slid off the edge of the bed, twisted sheets almost sending her face-first to the floor. "I hear you. I hear you!"

She struggled through the bedding.

"Who is it? What the hell do you want?"

One last bang rattled the hinges. She threw the door open and a man, his arms folded, stood before her, his silhouette enhanced by blinding sunlight. Katherine rubbed her eyes, trying to focus. "Oh, Joe it's you. I'm sorry."

"Yeah. It's me. Why haven't you come to work? The place is hopping and I'm up to my elbows."

"I don't feel like it."

"What?"

"I'm done working and if you don't mind, I need to be alone."

Geary stepped back. "When's that baby due?"

"Uh, December. I can't wait to get this damn thing out of me."

"You're awful big. Have you been to a doctor?"

"That's none of your business."

Geary ran his hand through his buzz-cut. Perplexed, he tried a little coaxing.

"You know, young lady," he said, "this ain't the end of the world. At some point, you'll have that young figure back." He retreated a few more steps and gestured with his arm. "Why don't you come to work? Remember how good it felt the first time?"

The first time! The first time! The ugly thought of Bob Kelly ramming her insides sent an explosion of nausea from her mouth. It landed at Geary's feet, splashing his shoes and pant legs. She coughed and wiped stray slop from her arm with the other arm. And like a Marine catching a fallen buddy, he caught her as her legs withered.

"Whoa there," he said. "I didn't know you were that bad." He eased her to bed, resting her head onto the pillow. "Let's get your legs up and take those sneakers off."

She sobbed, "I'm sorry, Joe. I, I don't know what happened. It felt like a giant rock hit me."

"You need rest. Forget about work."

He pulled a mop from the closet and cleaned the floor. His shoes and pants would have to wait. Katherine found herself watching him sway left then right, muscles rippled beneath a skin-tight tee shirt.

Maybe I can tell Joe the truth.

"Joe," she said. "I never thanked you."

"For what?"

"For protecting me from the man at the cash register."

"That bum?" He wrung the mop in the sink. "You'll never see him around here again after what happened that night."

"What night, the same night you threw him out?"

"Yeah. After we closed up and went to the cabins I heard some arguing. I went to check it out. It was some drunks parked down the road. One of 'em was that guy."

Katherine pulled the sheet to her chin. "What happened?"

"Nothing much," he said, not wanting to scare her. "They said their buddy ran out of gas and they were lookin' for 'em."

"What'd you do?"

"Let's just put it this way. They're not comin' back."

Her body shook under the sheet and a wild-eyed look took over.

"You getting sick again?" he said.

"I, I have to tell you something," she began, but the memory of Kelly's knife stopped her.

"What do wanna tell me?"

"You're right. I just need to rest."

"Listen to me. You take it easy until that baby's born."

"But what about working and free dinner?"

"Don't sweat that," he assured, stowing the mop. "I'll make sure you get all the food you need. I'll check on you later." Then he was gone.

The baby kicked. The image of Kelly raping her and her mother after stabbing her father played out in her head. *I'll never be able to tell anybody the truth.* She closed her eyes, but there was nothing to pray to. She had given up on God.

* * *

Originally, fifty people had volunteered to paint signs for the march on Archie's Barbershop, but half that number had shown. Not discouraged, Ben and his neighbors used black paint to print *NAACP-BATTLE HYMN-EQUAL RIGHTS FOR ALL* on thirty white placards.

With the task completed, Ben commented, "Dr. King will be proud of us." As the group dispersed, Ben shook hands and reminded each person, "Meet here at seven in the morning."

On the other side of midnight, lights went out in the Toony's apartment. Martha tossed in bed. Ben, first asleep, soon stirred. His arms flailed as he yelled, "Isaac! Isaac! Not you! No! Not you! Not you!" When he settled, Martha brushed sweat from his forehead until sunrise.

At 7:00 a.m., people began to arrive. Martha, her feet dragging, offered hot coffee to those helping one another tie strings that held their placards in place, one string looped around the neck the other around the waist.

Though only half the promised fifty people had shown the night before, seventy individuals now gathered. With not enough signs to go around, some folks scrawled their own message on scraps of cardboard that Ben supplied. *"Free Battle Hymn, Justice for All,"* and *"Cut My Hair-I Don't Bite"* were a few of the ad-hoc demands.

"Okay, okay, everyone listen up," said Ben, his arms raised.

The group quieted. As he surveyed his neighbors, a smile formed on his lips and his brow relaxed. "I know it's Tuesday," he chuckled, "but y'all dressed like Sunday." The group returned a breathy laugh. "Let's form our line and get on our way." He turned to Martha and kissed her cheek, "Take care of the store, sweetheart. I'll be back for dinner."

The line snaked along. A soft handclap kept time as a chant of *Freedom, Yeah Freedom,* traveled on a morning breeze. It was 7:45 when the group arrived downtown. Onlookers stepped aside, scratching heads in disbelief. Some faces expressed fear, for never had they witnessed so many blacks in a deliberate, unwavering procession.

In front of the barbershop, Ben instructed, "We want to loop and circle. Remember," he added, "we represent *all* of our people. Don't let anything cause you to raise your voice or lash out."

As he finished, protesters moved in a determined current. The group stretched five doors down the block, all the way to Gerber's front door. Not long after, a dozen Battle Hymn police cars and five paddy wagons arrived. They took up positions across the street, playing wait and see.

In the meantime, Archie parked his black Chevy in front of the shop. He looked at the line in disbelief.

Ben greeted him with, "I told you something would happen," and followed Archie as he waddled toward the picketers. The line broke enough to permit the two men's passage to the front door.

On the steps Archie turned and murmured, "Goddamn coloreds. Don't know your place." He spit on Ben's shoes. The rhythm of the march continued; the chant remained mournful and unyielding. Archie unlocked the door, went inside and switched on the barber pole.

The mill whistle blasted. Inside the shop Archie leaned toward the picture window and flipped Ben a middle finger. At the same time the window shattered, followed by the pop of gunfire. The blast echoed through the canyon of brick buildings lining downtown. Archie's body teetered. Along with shards of glass, he tumbled to the sidewalk, landing on his side. With one visible eye still open, blood poured from a gaping hole in the back of his skull. What seemed an eternity of silence erupted into screams. The protesters scattered. Ben knelt at Archie's side.

"Not this! My God. No!" he cried.

Police scrambled, chasing and clubbing any blacks they snagged. As Ben stood, a sharp blow knocked him to the ground, rendering him unconscious. He was thrown into one of the paddy wagons and hustled to police headquarters where he awoke early in the evening to a throbbing head and crusty, blood-matted hair. He could hear women's screams and men's shouts coming from some other part of the jail's three-story lock-up.

After fifteen minutes, a detective with two-days worth of stubble, a tired-looking suit jacket, and a half-spent cigarette dangling from his mouth, came to the cell. A stone-faced nurse stood at his side. Ben sat on the edge of the bunk while she treated his head wound. The detective chain-smoked and lingered in the corner, once in a while running a comb through his slick black hair. Sewer stench and the cop's secondhand smoke ran up Ben's nose, almost causing him to puke.

Five stitches later, the nurse left. The detective remained.

"Got you a real mess here," he began. "Looks like they're chargin' murder one. That means the chair."

Ben jerked upward, his head still beating, his eyes rheumy and bulging. "I didn't kill anyone," he mumbled.

"You better tell that to the dead barber who was laying at your feet when we caught you. And, by the way, I'm Wilcox. Detective Wilcox."

"I had nothing to do with that man's death," Ben replied, the stinky air and weight of Wilcox's words bringing him to his senses.

The detective sat on the bunk, lit another smoke and offered Ben a drag.

"No thanks," he answered.

"You might find nothing but time on your hands," Wilcox said. "They say suckin' smoke helps pass the time while you're waitin' to fry."

Ben laughed nervously, "You got it all wrong, Mister. We were just protesting because they wouldn't cut our hair. My group was peaceful."

"So you admit it was your idea," Wilcox said.

"What idea?"

"To organize Negroes to march downtown."

Realizing he was guilty by his own admission, Ben replied, "Yeah. It was my idea."

Wilcox stood. "I'll give you the night to think about that," he said, slamming the cell door.

"Where's my wife," Ben yelled.

"Her name Martha?"

"Yes."

"We told her to come back. You can see her before we bring you to see the judge."

"I didn't do anything," Ben pleaded, his face pressed to the bars.

"Oh, come on now," Wilcox laughed. "We got you for disorderly and paradin' without a permit. You said it yourself."

"What about the other charge," Ben begged.

"We'll just have to see what our fellas uncover now, won't we?"

Ben's grip wilted from the cell door. Terrified, he sat on the bunk.

29.

Geary rang up customers as Ron and O'Hara strolled through the front door. He acknowledged their arrival with raised eyebrows and, "Hey, gents. Grab a seat. I'll be right with you."

As usual, Ron sat in the private booth. O'Hara tagged along. Ron looked around the busy diner. There was no sign of Katherine.

Geary, a jovial monster now that business was booming, rubbed his hands like a jackpot winner. "O'Hara," he said. "Are you staying for a bite?"

"Nah," answered O'Hara. "I just wanna check on my girl."

"Where is she," Ron asked.

Geary slid into the booth, his voice hushed as if communicating affairs of state.

"Katherine didn't show for up work so I went to your cabin." He leaned back, stretched his arms full length. "I think she'll be needing bed rest."

"What do you mean," O'Hara asked, a hint of worry in his voice.

Geary drew upon knowledge gleaned from helping his physician-father and experiences during the war. "A lot of times when a girl's getting near delivery," his index finger stabbed the air, "she'll get a little blue or down-in-the-dumps. It's best to comfort them and see that they get their nourishment." Ron and O'Hara listened to every word. Geary continued, "Pregnant girls and how they feel? It's a rollercoaster of emotions, but they usually snap out of it after the baby comes."

O'Hara sighed. "Her mother went through it," he said. "I remember how she didn't want to see anybody or do anything. It lasted a few weeks, but after Katherine was born, she was as good as new."

As the armchair generals debated, Ron asked, "Is she gonna be okay?"

Geary swiped his palm over Ron's hair. "Right as rain, son," he assured. "Now, what do you want for dinner?"

"I've been thinking about meatloaf all day," Ron said, "but how we gonna pay?"

Geary chuckled. "It's a baby gift. You eat for free 'til you pass that test. Now, meatloaf it is. I'll make it two. You know *who* will be hungry."

O'Hara slid out the other end of the booth and adjusted his sidearm. "If you don't mind, fellas," he said, "I'll go visit my daughter."

* * *

Without warning, the door to cabin six flew open.

"I said don't bother me!" Katherine screamed.

"Now who do you think you're speaking to, young lady?"

"Da...Da...Daddy. I'm sorry. I thought you were someone else."

"Even if I was, that's not the way your mother and me brought you up," he scolded, doing a quick scan of the cabin's interior. "Are you going to invite me in or have you forgotten all your manners?"

She stepped aside. O'Hara soaked in the place his daughter called home. He avoided puke that remained after Geary's quick wash. There were garments strewn everywhere, some dirty, some clean. The garbage smelled.

She sat on the edge of the bed, her head hung in embarrassment.

"I can explain."

"Sweetheart, what's going on here? This isn't the way we live."

"I…my…I can't tell you," she sobbed as she stood and ran to his open arms. "Things are all wrong, Daddy. My head's full of awful things!"

O'Hara recalled the conversation about pregnant girls and the blues.

"It's all temporary, Katherine. When the baby comes, you'll feel different, trust me."

She bawled into his shirtsleeve. He caressed her shaking head. "Now, now, it's okay," he comforted. "Things will be fine. That's my girl. It's okay. Daddy's here."

Katherine looked to her father, a stream of tears running down her cheeks.

"I wish I could tell you," she whimpered. "I wish you knew."

"I understand, sweetheart. It's going to pass. You'll see." He stroked her greasy hair. "Do you want to reconsider coming home?"

"No." She swallowed hard. "My place is here."

Ron arrived and nudged open the cabin door with his leg, two plates of food stacked in his hands. "Here's dinner," he said. "Am I interrupting?"

"No, Ron, we're just sharing' a moment," O'Hara replied.

Katherine wiped her nose on her forearm.

"I'd best be on my way," O'Hara said. "Your mother will be wondering where I am." He kissed Katherine's cheek and looked around the cabin. "Clean this place up, please."

After O'Hara left, Ron put the plates on the cluttered bed.

"Why all teary eyed," he asked.

"I'm confused," she replied, "but it's none of your concern. Let's eat."

30.

A judge ordered Ben held over pending further
investigation into Archie's murder. The sheriff transported
him from a holding cell to the wing that housed full-fledged
criminals. There was no bail for suspected murderers, so
two weeks passed without contact from family or friends.
Finally, Martha was allowed a short visit. Though
distressed beyond her ability to eat or sleep, she smiled,
wore make-up and told him things were good at the store.
Yes, business is steady, everybody feels terrible about what
happened and the other protesters were fined but set free.
Detective Wilcox stopped by from time-to-time, reminding
Ben, "This could mean the Death House."

* * *

Ben slumped on his bunk, almost in a trance, gazing toward
Blue Mountain, visible through the window of his cage.
That day in early September, he observed Canada geese
gliding south, instinctively avoiding Battle Hymn's soot.
The jailer interrupted the peaceful moment, raking his key
ring over the bars.

"Visitor. Visitor," he announced like a town crier.

Ben thought, Martha? She's a day early.

He ironed his prison-issue shirt collar with his thumb
and a dab of spit. He tucked the oversized garment into his
trousers and cinched the belt to its last hole. The sheet-
metal mirror tacked to the cell's cinderblock wall reflected
an old wavy ghost. He ran his hand over his hair and

rubbed his face. After a splash of cold water, he murmured, "No time to shave."

The guard shouldered the cell door open. Ben sucked a deep breath and moved down the corridor, ignoring calls of 'Nigger, get outta here,' 'Put 'em with me,' and, 'I hear you goin' to the death house, tar-baby.'

The visitor ward, an inhospitable space featuring damp walls, dull linoleum floors and wooden tables with wire mesh dividers, was vacant except for Ben. Yellow and black posters instructing on the "dos" and "don'ts" of civilian-prisoner interface screamed for attention. The surly guard used a baton to nudge his prisoner to a table near the lone window.

For Ben, this visit was a conundrum of elation and embarrassment. He rubbed his sweat-shined palms over his denim pant legs, as the steel-plated visitor's door swung open.

"Ron! What in tarnation are you doing in this miserable cesspit?"

Ron smiled and sat across from Ben, whose hands were now pressed to the wire mesh, desperate for any form of contact with the outside world.

"Mr. Toony, I'm sorry I didn't come sooner," Ron said.

"Why did you come, son?"

"I have some news that you probably haven't heard."

Ben thrust his chin, "What news could you have for me?"

Ron pulled his chair close. "I spoke with Mr. O'Hara. You remember him, don't you?"

"I never met him," Ben replied, "but he's your father-in-law, right?"

"Yeah. He's also a mill cop."

"What's that got to do with me? Too bad he wasn't around to help Isaac." Ben wished he could stuff the last sentence back in his mouth.

Ron pressed on. "Officer O'Hara said he overheard conversation between two Battle Hymn detectives last week. They said they found a deer rifle on the roof of Kresge's Five and Dime. That building's two blocks west of Archie's Barbershop."

Ben's eyes brightened.

"They're conducting tests to determine if it's the same gun that killed Archie. If it's true, they can't charge *you* with murder."

Ben's water-laden eyelids could hold no more. "Oh, sweet Jesus." he cried. "Please make it so, dear Lord. Make it so."

Ron pressed his palms to the mesh in an effort to comfort his friend.

"No contact with the prisoner." the guard warned.

"Mr. Toony," Ron whispered. "I wish I never asked you to take us in that night. Isaac would still be alive if it weren't for me."

Ben looked to Ron as a father to a son.

"Ronald," he said, "it wasn't you or anything involving your situation. It was pure evil and there's not much any of us can do about that other than fight it." His head bowed. "That's how I ended up in this godforsaken place."

The guard banged his baton against a radiator. "Time!" he shouted then strode to Ben. "Let's go, boy. Party's over."

The light seemed to drain from Ben's eyes. "Thanks for taking the time to let me know about what your heard," he said. The guard jabbed the baton into the base of his spine. "Get a move on."

31.

Labor Day meant drunks three deep inside the Dublin Bar –
most of them steel mill dockworkers and Bob Kelly
sycophants.

"I have a dream, can ya believe it?" Kelly stretched his
arms in mockery of the crucifixion. "When we're done with
that King guy, he'll feel more like Nigger Jesus. Right,
men?" The majority cheered. Others chugged their drinks
and left. Kelly stood on his barstool.

"Hey, where the hell's Duffy?" he shouted.

"I don't know," someone replied.

At that moment, Duffy shuffled through the door
wringing his hands, his face drawn.

"Duffy," Kelly screamed, "get ya'r sagging ass over
here." Kelly jumped to the floor and pulled two chairs from
a stack near the dartboard. "Leave us a little room to
breathe, will ya guys?"

The gang returned to the bar. The pair sat in a huddle.
Kelly placed his hand on the small of Duffy's neck. He
pulled him close enough to drink his spittle.

"Did ya get it," Kelly demanded.

"I finally got the damn key, Bob. But when I reached the
roof, it was gone. There were buckets of tar and tarpaper all
over the fuckin' place. They must be re-doin' the roof."

Kelly waited a beat, his breathing grew rapid, and the
grip on Duffy's neck tightened.

"Ya dumb fuck. I told ya not to get hammered before ya
took care of that spook. Now look at the mess we're in. Ya

panicked and left the gun there, ya dumb shit. Ya better hope one of those idiot roofers found it and not the cops."

"I wore gloves, Bob. There's no fingerprints."

"Prints? Who gives a royal shit about prints? If the Battle Hymn Police get hold of it, we'll have a big problem."

Duffy cowered. "What problem?"

"Did ya ever think that there's a serial number on the gun? Did it occur to ya that when I bought it, the store might have registered the goddamn thing?"

Kelly relinquished the neck-hold.

Duffy supported his head in his hands. "I'm sorry. I fucked up."

Kelly's brow sharpened. "Not only did ya screw that up. Ya missed. You killed the wrong guy. That black son of a bitch is still alive."

"I swear to God I had his head right in the crosshairs. I don't know what happened."

"Ya missed, dip shit. That's what happened. And now we gotta lay low and hope for the best."

Kelly sat back and observed his partner's shrinking image. "Ah, come on," he said. "We all mess up from time to time. Don't let it get ya down. If those cops were so smart they would've nailed me years ago. C'mon, let's get a snoot full."

"Two doubles," Kelly shouted, the crowd gathering around them. The pair downed the whiskeys in a single gulp. "Another. Another."

Duffy looked like he was about to puke.

"Another?" he asked, looking toward the exit.

* * *

Ben slept despite the howls of inmates and the stench that came with each breath. In the morning, a rapid tap-tap awoke him just after sunrise. He rubbed his crusty eyes.

"Who in God's name is it," he yawned.

Detective Wilcox, dressed in the same crumpled black suit, leaned against the cell door slapping his badge on the bars.

"Gonna be a bright day, ain't it," he teased, sipping a hot coffee.

"May I have a little privacy," asked Ben, as he rolled out of bed.

"You seen one prisoner piss, you seen 'em all," Wilcox replied.

Ben wagged his head in disbelief and did his business through a hole in the floor. After zipping his trousers, he came to the bars.

"Had your fun, Mister," he prodded.

"Hey, don't get wise," the detective said. "I'm here to save your ass."

"Yeah, right."

"Listen," Wilcox shot back. "You got that murder-one hanging over you and today you're gonna be arraigned."

Ben supported himself with a two-handed grip on the bars, his forehead pressed to the cold-rolled steel.

"I didn't do it," he murmured.

"Maybe not, but maybe yes," Wilcox whispered. "What's important is you're a Negro and that's the way it is. The DA is pressing hard. You never know what he might say. He could say something like you popped Archie with a pistol and passed the gun to one of your boogie brothers. Or he might get creative and say something like a… you jumped through the window and strangled Archie with a towel then dragged him to the sidewalk and stomped on his head." Wilcox touched his chin. "If I recall, the only witness to the shooting were your black friends and their testimony won't mean anything in front of a white jury. And besides, you had blood all over your shoes and pant legs. But no matter, Archie's a dead white man, you're the live black one who was standing close enough to kill him, and we both know how that story ends."

Ben sat on the bunk, hands folded in his lap, deciding whether to reveal the information Ron had delivered. Wilcox lit a cigarette and slid the butt through the bars.

"You want a drag," he asked.

Ben raised his hands, "No."

After a minute, Wilcox asked, "I think the DA will make you a deal if you're willing to play ball."

Ben's eyes widened. "Deal? What deal?"

Wilcox cleared his throat as he leaned on the cell door.

"If you plead guilty to the protest and parading without a permit, he thinks he can make this murder thing go away."

"How's he gonna do that?"

"Well, the DA asked me to pass this along. He told me to tell you that they found a rifle on the roof of the five and dime. The ballistics test matches it with the slug that killed the barber."

Ben concealed his heart almost leaping from his chest.

"Yeah, and what does that mean," he asked.

"You're stupid, aren't you," Wilcox replied, crushing the cigarette with the heel of his shoe, immediately lighting another. "The DA wants to know who really pulled that trigger and it means you'll serve ninety days, idiot, then go home. That is, only if you plead guilty to being there and having no permit."

Wilcox leaned against the cell door and laughed. "Don't you understand," he said. "After watching you coloreds run around loose and all, the DA's office has to show something for all our efforts or else the good taxpayers of

Battle Hymn will think we've been wasting their time and money."

"You call that's saving my ass?"

"No. This is. And you'd better listen up." Wilcox readjusted his lapel. "The ballistics boys discovered that whoever fired the weapon was smart enough to wear gloves. There were no prints, but the knucklehead didn't know how to sight a gun. The crosshairs were too high."

"And so," asked Ben.

"And so, it was probably your head he was lookin' to bust open like a watermelon. Not Archie's. If it weren't for that fact we'd be holding you on conspiracy charges. If he wanted to, the DA could say you hired someone to pull the trigger, but since it looks like you were the target..." He smiled. "We couldn't hold you on false charges, now. Could we?"

"Oh, dear Lord," Ben cried out. "This world's gone mad!"

"I don't know much about the world," Wilcox said, "but I'll tell you what. You'll be safer here in jail. Ever since that King guy made his speech in front of the Washington Memorial, there's a lot of pissed-off, trigger-happy white guys roaming the country. Some of them are right here in town."

Ben covered his ears with his hands, trying to block the detective's words. Wilcox aimed smoke rings toward Ben's eyes. "I tell you something, though," he continued. "You should consider yourself lucky. When that judge passes sentence, you'll be able to hide out in here until..." He counted his fingers. "Um, let me see here. That'll be...Yeah. You'll be outta this place sometime in November, if you mind your behavior. Maybe some of the hotheads will have cooled their heels by then."

Wilcox glanced at his watch. "The guards are comin' for you in a few hours." He flicked the half-spent cigarette to the floor. "Remember. Give the DA what he wants. Plead guilty and count your lucky stars."

The jailhouse trustee rolled a cart to Ben's cell.

"Chow," he announced, slipping a tin dish of grits, beans and cornbread through a slot in the door.

"Guilty," Wilcox whispered then left.

The porter snatched the discarded cigarette. He offered Ben a hit. Ben pushed it away.

"Suit yourself," the trustee laughed, as he rolled his cart to the next cell.

* * *

An hour later, propping his flaccid figure against the wall, a guard perused the comic section of the newspaper while Ben shaved. With *Nancy, the Phantom* and *Superman* under his belt, the guard became restless.

"Come on," he whined. "Let's get a move on."

Ben ran a starched towel over his face.

"I'm ready," he said, offering his arms to be cuffed.

"I don't care 'bout that shit," the guard replied, his hand planted firmly on the butt of a .38. "Get your black ass in gear."

The men walked to the corridor that connected the justice department to the prison.

"Stop here," the guard yelled.

He jabbed his baton in Ben's gut, never losing contact. The court bailiff came into the corridor.

"Okay, Marty," the bailiff said. "This guy's mine from here on."

A few minutes later, they arrived at the prisoner holding room. The bailiff opened the door and poked his head in.

"Okay to enter," he asked.

"Bring him," came the nonchalant response.

He used the baton to push Ben forward.

The room, a twelve-foot by twelve-foot plaster cubbyhole with pale green walls, a small table, four chairs and a single light fixture hanging from the ceiling, served as the attorney-defendant conference area.

The second bailiff stood in the corner, sleepy-eyed, arms folded across his chest. A fresh-faced young man wearing a crisp suit and tie sat the table. Ben sat across from him.

"Mr. Toony," the man asked.

"Yeah."

"I'm John Shea."

"What do you want," Ben asked as Martha entered the room through a second door.

"I'm your lawyer."

Ben's attention was drawn to his wife. She, dressed in a dark blue suit topped off with a pillbox hat, rushed to his side.

"Benjamin!"

Ben stood, afraid to touch her, for prison dirtiness clung to him. She took his hand and rubbed it over her cheek.

"Ben, my love, don't be ashamed," she whispered as they sat across from the attorney.

"Mr. Toony, we only have a few minutes," the lawyer said.

"I understand, sir," Ben replied. "What do you want?"

"You've got to make a plea on the two charges. One's a simple misdemeanor. The other carries a death sentence."

At that, Martha clenched Ben's hand.

"I intend to plead you not guilty on all charges," the attorney continued.

"May I have a moment with my wife," Ben said.

"Make it quick," the attorney's hands flailing. "This is no joke. There're people who want you to fry."

"I know. But just give us a minute."

"Okay."

The attorney retired to a corner of the room, panting nervously. Ben pulled Martha to a whisker's length.

"Honey," he began, "I got word that they found evidence that'll prove I didn't kill anybody." Martha squeezed his hand even tighter. "All I got to do is plead guilty to demonstrating without a permit," he continued. "But there's a catch," he added as his head dipped. "I've gotta serve ninety days."

"Oh, Ben," she whispered. "Do it. In God's name, do it."

"That's my plan, sweetheart."

"But what about this lawyer," she asked.

"I'll deal with him."

Ben waved the lawyer to the table.

"Mr. Shea," he said, "I wanna plead guilty to the protest charge."

Shea stepped back, unsure of how to respond. Finally, he spoke.

"Why on earth would you do that?"

"I got word from two independent sources that a gun was found," Ben replied. "One of my sources is a detective named Wilcox. The other is a friend."

"What friend?" Martha whispered.

Ben continued, "Wilcox says if I plead guilty to the protest charge, they'll drop the murder charge."

Shea's head shook in disbelief.

"What? Are you crazy? Don't you see what that cop is trying to do?"

Ben frowned.

"Listen to me and listen good," the lawyer said. "When you plead guilty, you'll be admitting that you were there, standing right in front of that barber when he was murdered."

Ben stammered, "Ah...Ah...Ah..."

The lawyer kept rolling. "I have it on good information that there are several witnesses prepared to testify that you came by that barbershop a few weeks earlier and threatened Archie. They said you said, 'Something's gonna happen.' Do you recall that?"

"Yes," Ben admitted.

"You see what I'm saying about Wilcox? He's trying to box you in."

"But the detective told me they conducted tests that prove I couldn't have killed Archie."

"Are you willing to put your life in the hands of a slick cop looking to crack a case?"

"No," Ben answered. "But I believe my friend and my gut tells me to follow the detective's advice."

"Have it your way," Shea replied. "But when they stick that murder charge, you won't be thinking about ninety days. It'll be more like a six-by-six on death row."

Martha shivered. Ben warmed her, running his hands over her shoulders.

She whispered, "Benjamin?"

"I know what I'm doing," he assured her.

The clerk opened the door to the courtroom.

"We're ready," she said.

The lawyer collected his briefcase and led the way. Inside, Ben sat at the defense table, his wife in the row behind. Looking among the faces of curiosity seekers and family members of other defendants scheduled to appear on various charges, Ben noticed Wilcox lounging in the back row.

"All rise," the clerk commanded as the big-eyed judge, entered and sat behind the bench.

"Let's get going," he said. The clerk handed him the day's docket. "Okay, Benjamin Toony?"

Ben stood, as did the attorney, "Yes, your honor."

"You're here to be arraigned on two charges. The first is illegal protest and parading which carries a ninety-day sentence. How do you plead?"

Time seemed to stand still. Ben turned to Martha, her face blank, and her head nodding in slow motion. Ben captured a glimpse of Wilcox. A cigarette protruded from his lips as he gave a subtle wink.

"Well, Mr. Toony. I don't have all day. How do you plead?"

"Guilty, your honor."

"Okay," the judge puttered. "That resolves that." He flipped through several sheets of paper. "Ninety days and credit for time served," he said.

"The prisoner release date is November twentieth. All other matters pertaining to this defendant are dismissed."

Martha bawled her joy. Ben reached for her, but the bailiff whisked him from the courtroom. Shea, alone at the defense table, stood in disbelief. After stuffing papers into his briefcase, he made a hasty retreat from the courtroom, Wilcox hot on his heels.

32.

Boredom. Fumes. O'Hara couldn't differentiate between the two while languishing at the truck entrance. But a call from Captain Sullivan woke him up.

"O'Hara, you gotta get to my office before quittin' time."

"Aye, aye, Captain. I'll be there."

Ten minutes before the whistle, he sped off in the direction of corporate headquarters. Along the way he pondered, *Now what?*

"Come in. Come in. It's good to see you." Sullivan grinned, lounging in a new high-back leather chair. He waved his hand toward the wooden bench along the wall.

"Have a seat."

"Thanks, Captain."

With a sudden breath, Sullivan sprang from the seat, sucked his gut in, and paced the room.

"I'm sorry," he said. "I haven't had a flick of time to come by and visit you out there at that truck gate. How goes it, anyway?"

"Tolerable at best, Captain."

"Well, that's part of the reason I brought you here this afternoon." The captain produced a silver flask from the top drawer. "Join me?"

"Nah. None for me, sir."

"Oh, yeah, I forgot. You're on duty," Sullivan snickered before tossing back a capful. "Ah!" he declared. "Now there's heaven."

"What can I do for you, Captain," asked O'Hara, shifting on the bench.

The captain flopped in his expensive seat and propped his feet on the desk.

"It's time to shuffle the deck. I've got to move some of the guys around. Orders from the brass." He pointed toward the hallway. O'Hara remained silent. "Well, don't you want to know where *you'll* be workin'?"

Making a stab, O'Hara replied, "The main gate?"

"Right you are."

O'Hara concealed his disappointment. It would be difficult to visit his daughter while checking badges at the main gate.

"I didn't wanna bring this up, but I have no choice," Sullivan added.

"What is it, Captain?"

"Well, I know you carry an unloaded weapon."

O'Hara stammered, "I…I…can…"

"Save your words, lad. There's no need to explain," Sullivan said, as he popped from his seat again, supporting his weight with hands planted on the desk. "The problem is," he continued, "the big boys in the front office don't care. You see, after that colored riot and the dead barber, the company's takin' no chances. Every guard who's checkin' credentials has to have their weapon loaded and ready. No exceptions."

"I …I… c…can explain."

"I told you, no need. Ol' Sullivan's got you covered."

"Whaddya mean, Captain?"

"Here's how it's gonna work. You'll be in that old trailer," Sullivan continued, "next to the guard house. The other guards will do all the dirty work." He waved a warning finger. "You'll have to wear your sidearm, though.

But because you're in that cruddy trailer, no one'll stop by to check if your gun's loaded and neither will I. Okay?"

O'Hara replied, "Thank you, Captain. You've been good to me all these years."

Sullivan walked to the window. He pushed apart the Venetian blinds with his fingertips and looked to the parking lot.

"John," he lamented as the slats snapped shut, "I know you've been judged because of one mistake made years ago. I also know how some of the guys tease you and accuse you of being...Well, let's just say less than brave. "

"Captain," O'Hara interrupted, "What I did haunts me from the moment my eyes open. I should've never lent my gun to a friend. I can only hope that when my time comes I'll be forgiven."

"Hell would be busy if guys like you, who've asked for forgiveness, are condemned to the fire," Sullivan replied as he returned to his seat and took another belt from the flask.

"Captain," O'Hara asked, "when do I have to show up at the main gate?"

"End of the month, Johnny. That'll give you two more weeks with the squad car."

How will Ron get back to the Cloverleaf, O'Hara wondered. And what about Katherine? "Thanks again, Captain."

"Oh. There's one more thing."

"Yes, Captain."

"I know you've been visiting your daughter at lunch from time-to-time and giving her man a lift to those shacks at the end of the day."

O'Hara opened his mouth, but Sullivan cut him off. "You can do what you want with that car for two more weeks. I don't give a flyin' hoot. And when you turn it in, I'll get that boy a ride to the diner at the end of the day, don't worry." Sullivan's whiskey-flushed face blossomed a quarter-moon smile. "It's like I said. Ol' Sullivan's got you covered."

O'Hara took his hand. "Thank you, Captain."

"How's your daughter doing?"

"The baby's due around Christmas." O'Hara beamed.

"That'll be a great gift for your family during the most sacred season."

"I know, Captain. Mrs. O'Hara and me are very excited."

"Okay. Off you go. I gotta finish up."

* * *

O'Hara fired up the squad car. He drove to the desolate stretch of highway connecting the truck entrance to the Cloverleaf. After passing through the security gate and waving to the nightshift, he drove midway to the diner before pulling off the road and into a dirt lane.

Hidden by tall reeds, he cut the engine and laid his sidearm in his lap. He popped open the chamber and stared at six empty slots, massaging the barrel with his free hand. His eyes widened and narrowed as he delved into the past one painful memory at a time. He tightened his grip on the weapon as the scene – described to him by police investigating the death of his friend – played out in his head. *How could I have been so stupid, so careless? I'm responsible for the death of that man. I lost my career and put my wife through hell.*

He slipped a bullet from the cartridge loop, and spun the chamber, the doubled-load shell – designed to pass through a brick wall – rested between his thumb and index finger. His jaw clenched enough to crack the fillings of his bottom teeth. I'm not a coward, he thought. I can do this.

The chamber and bullet were milled to the highest specs; one should fit the other like a second skin. But no matter how hard O'Hara tried, his hand would not comply. He could not load the weapon. He shook, his neck muscles tightened. *Oh, Jesus God in heaven, what's wrong with me?* A second attempt brought the same result, as did the third and fourth. He made one final effort.

It grew dark. And, as trucks whizzed by, no-one noticed the squad car parked ten feet into weeds and the officer, his head slumped to the steering wheel, crying.

33.

Mrs. O'Hara folded clothes that had long ago lost their luster to the gray air of Battle Hymn. Mr. O'Hara sat at the kitchen table, staring at a pork chop.

"I'm worried about Katherine," she said.

"You're worried," he said, shoving his plate to the center of the table. "I used to see her everyday and one thing I can tell you, she's not our little girl anymore. Ron's no help either. His only concern is passing the damn test. He doesn't see how she's gone to hell in a hand basket."

Mrs. O'Hara stopped folding and went to the kitchen sink. She ran cold water over her raw palms. "We've got to do something."

"I've tried every which way." He sighed. "But she won't come home."

"Now that you've lost the car, we can't keep an eye on her," she admitted, coming to his side.

"I know, sweetheart. It's killin' me."

Mrs. O'Hara returned to her monotone laundry. "I'm not going to stand by and watch her become some form of, of, trailer trash."

Her husband stood and gave her a reassuring embrace. "There, there, Elizabeth. We raised her to be a Catholic. Besides, after the baby comes, and when Ron finally gets workin' as an electrician, he'll get her out of that hole and into a decent house. You'll see."

"How can you be so sure?"

"I've grown to know Ron, and it's like you said to me months ago. He loves Katherine.

* * *

As she fell asleep, Mrs. O'Hara took comfort in her husband's words. But after an hour, she awoke sweating. *There's a gaping hole in Katherine's life.* This thought caused her head to ache. In the morning, after getting her husband off to work, she pondered her daughter's condition.

The bed was made, corners clean and crisp. Breakfast dishes were washed and dried. She lugged the ironing board from a closet in the hallway and set up shop in the kitchen, prepared to spend the morning giving her husband's uniforms the military finish he required.

Steam shot from the front of the iron onto Mr. O'Hara's shirt. Her head pounded, but she pressed on, one shirt after another. When she was done, six shirts hung in a neat row. Next: six pairs of trousers. She mindlessly plucked a pair from the wicker basket when the idea came to her.

"No one's ever celebrated Katherine being pregnant," she murmured. "It's always been a curse. The poor girl never had a baby shower because her friends disowned her for marrying outside the Church." She flattened the first pair of pants on the board.

"That's what I'll do," she whispered to the iron. "I'll have a baby shower." *But Katherine won't come here. Well, we'll just go there. That's what we'll do. We'll throw a party in her cabin.*

The iron cut a sharp crease in the first pant leg. She set the second inseam. "But who's the *we* going to be? Surely, her father can't go," she whispered. "It wouldn't be a true baby shower with men present." As she finished the first pair of pants, another idea hit her.

I've got it. I know who'll come with me to the party. Oh thank you Blessed Virgin. Why didn't I think of that earlier?

* * *

The red soot ensconced between cracked floorboards
proved difficult to remove. Mrs. Magee worked the
broomstick as if it were an uncooperative dance partner, her
mother of pearl skin flubbing a beat behind. She persevered
until every flake of iron ore was swept from the porch and
onto the grass, which cost her most of the morning. With
that task completed, she wiped her brow with a corner of
the apron cinched to her hefty waist and turned her
attention to the potted mums.

"Are ya thirsty," she inquired of the bright orange and
yellow flowers. A few seconds later she replied, "Okay,
okay. Hold your goddamn horses. I've got to fill the
bucket." She shuffled to a rickety table and took hold of an
empty watering can. "You see, kids," she said, turning the
spout to the ground, "nothing's in it. Mother's got to fill it."
As she turned to enter the house, the noon whistle blasted.

"Lunch already? I'm running late."

Footsteps crunched on the battered walkway. Mrs.
Magee turned around. "Well," she said, "what in the
Queen's name brings you to this part of Wood Street."

"Top of the day, Mrs. Magee," replied Mrs. O'Hara.
"I've come to see Margaret Kelly. Is she in?"

"Suppose so. The poor woman barely leaves the house
anymore, ever since… Knock on the door. You'll find her
in there." She retreated to fill the water bucket.

"Thank you," said Mrs. O'Hara as she tapped the
diamond-shaped glass.

Though it was noon, drapes in the Kelly house were
drawn. The door creaked as it opened and Mrs. Kelly's
tired face filled the void. With it, the odor of dirty clothes
and cigarette smoke escaped into the mid-day air. Mrs.
O'Hara struggled not to hold her nose and close her eyes.
She caught a glimpse of Mrs. Kelly's bird-print dress –

robins, blue birds and cardinals. Their once brilliant colors had become innocent victims of the soot and smog war.

"Yeah. What do you want," said Mrs. Kelly.

"It's me, Elizabeth O'Hara."

"Oh," replied Mrs. Kelly. "Oh, dear me! Just a moment, I'll be right back."

The door slammed shut. Mrs. O'Hara heard her scramble to the back of the house. A few minutes later, Mrs. Kelly returned, gently reopening the door.

"What brings you here," she said, her voice wavering. "Are the kids alright?"

"That's why I'm here, Margaret."

"What's happened? What's wrong? Is it Ron?" Mrs. Kelly trembled.

"Nothing's wrong, not exactly. May I come in?"

Meanwhile, Magee drew uncomfortably close.

Mrs. Kelly, a hand to her temple, said, "Well, I don't know. I wasn't expecting company. The place is a mess."

"I promise not to take much of your time, Margaret. I need to ask you a favor."

Mrs. Kelly looked over her shoulder into the dark hallway. "I guess it'd be okay," she said. "But don't mind the clutter."

"Not to worry. We've all had days when the house wasn't as tidy as we'd like," Mrs. O'Hara said.

With that, Mrs. Kelly opened the door and Mrs. O'Hara stepped into a Protestant home for the first time. Mrs. Kelly directed her to the living room. Though each house on the street was designed and constructed by the same company – cookie cutters the architects called them – Mrs. O'Hara found the place foreign. There was no statue of the Blessed Virgin on the mantle or pictures of Jesus and the apostles hanging upon the wall. No holy water to bless guests. But there were blue-collar icons, work boots and grimy work clothes balled in the corridor leading to the kitchen. A crumpled, red wool blanket covered half the couch.

"I'm sorry," she apologized then snatched the cover, gesturing for Mrs. O'Hara to sit.

Mrs. O Hara opted for a chair. "Margaret," she began, resting her palms on her knees, "we're going to be grandparents. It's a happy event in any family."

Mrs. Kelly sat on the couch across from her guest, its once white lace now dingy grey.

"I've not given it much thought," she muttered. "I'm afraid to."

"What on earth of? They're just young people. They're searching for happiness."

"Don't be naïve," said Mrs. Kelly.

"It's us who's naïve," retorted Mrs. O'Hara. "These kids don't care about the nonsense that's pitted us against one another. Soon we'll be relics."

Mrs. O'Hara read the doubt in Mrs. Kelly's eyes.

"It'll happen. Just wait and see. Our children and grandchildren," she continued, "they'll look back and wonder what in God's name were those old people thinking."

Mrs. O'Hara scanned pictures on wall behind the couch. Her emotions rose, her eyes glistened at the sight of Ron in a baby carriage, taking a pony ride along the river, Mr. Kelly carrying his son on his shoulders in waist-deep snow.

"I know things are changing," Mrs. Kelly said. "But not Ron's father. He lives in the past. You know how it is. I have no choice. I've got to live there with him."

Mrs. O'Hara searched her handbag. "I understand," she replied, wiping her eyes with a yellow hanky. "My John's done stupid things in the past and I live with the consequences every day."

After a round of nose blowing and sniffles, Mrs. Kelly said, "Why are you here?"

Mrs. O'Hara stuffed the hanky in her purse and snapped it shut.

"It's Katherine. She's going to have the baby near Christmas and I'm worried about her. She and Ron live at the old truck stop. You know the one. It's out on the road that leads to the back entrance of the mill."

Mrs. Kelly gasped. "You don't mean that old whorehouse, do you?"

"It's not like that anymore," assured Mrs. O'Hara. "An ex-Marine is fixing the place up and turning it into a decent diner. And those cabins where… Well, those cabins have been cleaned and fumigated. The only thing Mr. Geary – that's his name – hasn't been able to change is the reputation."

"You still haven't told me why you're here."

"I want to give my daughter a baby shower."

"A baby shower," Mrs. Kelly repeated. "That's a terrific idea. We can go downtown to Jordan's department store. They have all sorts of things for mothers-to-be."

Like scheming schoolgirls, the women sat side by side on the ratty couch. "I can't breathe a word of this to Bob," Mrs. Kelly whispered.

"Of course not," said Mrs. O'Hara.

"When do you want to do it? Is it a surprise?"

"A surprise is the only way to go. We can hail a cab during the day when our men are at the mill. Katherine is usually in her cabin. It'll be a grand surprise." Mrs. O'Hara folded her hands as if praying.

"Let's meet at Jordan's tomorrow," said Mrs. Kelly. "When we've finished shopping, we can find a taxi right in front of the store."

Mrs. O'Hara lamented, "Why couldn't it be like this all the time?"

"I don't know. Maybe it's like you said. Forty or fifty years from now we'll be relics and so will these old ways."

Mrs. Kelly walked Mrs. O'Hara to the door.

"I'll see you at noon in front of Jordan's," she whispered, tilting her head to the wall. "My neighbor's like a telegraph. I don't want her to know what we're up to. She might tell Bob."

"I understand," said Mrs. O'Hara, speaking softly, taking hold of Mrs. Kelly's hand. "Tomorrow at noon."

Mrs. O'Hara walked onto the porch. The wood creaked. She came face-to-face with Mrs. Magee, who groused, "You people never learn, do you? You should keep to your own kind."

34.

The next the morning, Mrs. O'Hara dropped the hat on her husband's head, and stuffed a lunchbox under his arm.

"Now off you go," she said with a nudge in the back. "Have a grand day," she waved as he moved to the sidewalk. When he was out of sight she went to the kitchen.

On a shelf above the sink sat a Chock Full O' Nuts coffee can. In it was a piece of paper, the list she made during the night while Mr. O'Hara slept. On the list were items for Katherine and necessities for the baby. Though there was no way of knowing boy or girl, something told her that her grandchild would be a boy. A strong, beautiful and healthy boy, she thought. Maybe they'll name him John.

* * *

Jordan's, a four-story department store the size of a city block, was an expensive place to shop. Most of its clientele were the wives of wealthy steel mill executives. Mrs. O'Hara considered this as she reached into her bottom drawer where underwear, slips and bras resided. After some rummaging, she produced a tattered envelope.

She fingered the small wad of five-dollar bills – money skimmed from the household budget. Building a reserve fund had been a project in the works for several years, something for a rainy day, a safety net for a family that walked the blue-collar tight rope.

At first, she removed two fives, balled them in her fist and put them in her purse. But after some thought, she tore into the envelope, stashing the remaining bills with the other two.

* * *

Mrs. O'Hara started out on the two-mile walk with a smile, but by the time she reached downtown, her feet were blistered, her used black pumps almost a half-size too big.

Things were getting moist beneath her second-hand blue wool skirt and matching top. She nervously adjusted her white clip-on earrings, shifting the patent leather clutch from one hand to another. As she neared the hustle-bustle in front of Jordan's, her girdle nagged, but she ignored its bite, wanting nothing more than to blend in. She alternated glances between the sidewalk, the street and the faces of passersby, hoping whoever had donated her once expensive outfit to the clothing drive wouldn't come strolling down the block.

As the noon whistle sounded, she massaged her soles, shifting weight from one foot to another. All the while, she searched the field of faces. No sign of Mrs. Kelly.

Limousines pulled to the curb. She stood in awe. Wives of steel mill bosses, dressed to impress, emerged prepared to shop the day away. Beefeater-styled attendants, who opened the store's magnificent gold-trimmed doors as if each woman were a queen, greeted these Grand Dames.

Fifteen minutes passed. Once more, she scanned the mid-day crowd. Still no Mrs. Kelly. Exasperated, she approached the store's entrance and the giant doors swung inward followed by, "Welcome to Jordan's." The rich baritone equaled the opulence of its costumed owner.

A raspy voice yelled, "Hey, O'Hara! I'm over here!"

Mrs. Kelly stood on her tiptoes, raw heels exposed from the backs of sensible flats in need of a polish. Her black and white checkerboard dress swayed with each frantic wave, her thick roan hair pulled to an unyielding bun.

"Oh, there you are." Mrs. O'Hara sighed.

"You look like a million bucks," Mrs. Kelly offered.

"As do you."

"This?" She smirked. "This was my mother's. She gave it to me when Bob and I got hitched."

Mrs. O'Hara switched gears. "Where are the baby gifts?"

"Third floor," interrupted a tuxedoed gentleman. "The elevators are to your left." He sniffed the carnation attached to his lapel and extended his arm toward the bank of ornate wood-carved doors.

"Thanks, Geeves," replied Mrs. Kelly.

The women walked arm-in-arm to the elevators, waiting with other shoppers, mostly women who jockeyed for position.

"Isn't this place magnificent," Mrs. O'Hara whispered.

"Yeah, it sure is," replied Mrs. Kelly, her voice two notches louder than necessary. "Before Ron came along, I used to walk through this ritzy place for sheer entertainment," she continued. "I couldn't afford a darn thing, mind ya, but it was a pleasure to see beautiful stuff."

The two women held hands. When the elevator door opened, they were nudged in the shoulders, herded forward like cattle.

"Next stop, second floor," announced the operator, his bright red uniform accented his dark skin, and his silky voice. "Toiletries, lingerie, junior sportswear, shoes for the lady, 'n' Jordan's Fur Salon."

He slid a bronze lever to the right and the heavy door closed. Inside the elevator, wood panels shined. Meanwhile, waves of perfume flooded the ten-by-ten rising box.

After gliding to a halt, he announced, "Lets 'em out, lets 'em out!"

The impatient crowd parted to allow half the passengers their exit. Another handful filled the void.

"Back away, ladies," he called as the door shut. "Next stop, third floor, children's wear 'n' toys, casual 'n' formal dress for teens, linens 'n' beddin', carpetin' for the home, maternity 'n' items for the baby."

A short ride later, the door opened.

"Steps aside, steps aside," he cautioned. Mrs. Kelly and Mrs. O'Hara wiggled their way through immovable passengers and onto the third floor.

"That was a battle," said Mrs. O'Hara.

"You're telling me," replied Mrs. Kelly. She pressed one hand to her forehead, the other to her nose.

The women, intoxicated by everything Jordan's, stood silent.

"Over there," Mrs. Kelly said. "That's where the baby stuff is."

She dragged Mrs. O'Hara by the hand. Along the way, they passed fashion displays. Each design spared no detail. Mannequins were expensively garbed, complete with painted on smiles, makeup and human hair down to the eyelashes.

Mrs. O'Hara's heart soared. *Maybe our grandchild will unite us.*

"Here we are." Mrs. Kelly's arm swept the air. "Get a load of this place."

Suspended from the high ceiling were dozens of wooden, pearl-white storks. In each of their yellow beaks hung a white diaper. Each contained a life-size rubber baby. Over on the east side of the room, shafts of sunlight burst through giant windowpanes. Twinkling piano music added sparkle to the ten thousand square foot space. In the center, racks of maternity outfits divided by trimesters ran north to south. In another section, on countertops stretched along white plaster walls, were outfits so small they appeared suited for a toy instead of a human. There were other displays that featured rattles, bibs, blankets, diaper bags and safety pins with stork heads, some pink, some baby blue.

Floor attendants assisted well-to-do women who fussed whether the five hundred dollar pram or two hundred dollar silver spoon with matching bowl were suitable gifts. The two blue-collar wives and their second-hand outfits stood out.

Mrs. Kelly steered clear of pricey items.

"This way," she said as she walked toward a basketful of booties, pajamas, knitted hats and bibs. "We can find some cheap stuff here."

Mrs. O'Hara joined her. "Aren't these darling," she cooed, as she held a pair of knit booties to her rouged cheeks.

"They're wonderful. But what color should we get? Pink? Blue?"

Mrs. O'Hara clutched the tiny boots to her heart. "It's going to be a boy," she said, "I just know it."

"You seem dead certain."

"I know it's strange, but somehow, I *know* it's going to be a boy."

"Well, a boy would be grand. Someone to carry on the family name." Mrs. Kelly grabbed a shopping bag from a nearby dispenser. "Will you look at this," she said, dangling the white and gold paper sack. "It must cost a fortune to make these things."

Mrs. Kelly took the booties from Mrs. O'Hara and placed them in the bag. "Oh, and by the way," she struggled for the next words, "I...I only have...five bucks."

"Don't worry. I've been saving for something like this," replied Mrs. O'Hara, her eyes fixed on the beige carpet. After a few uncomfortable moments, she raised her chin and noticed shame in Mrs. Kelly's eyes. She took her by the arm. "Don't be embarrassed," she said. "Your being here is worth all the saints in heaven."

"Yeah, a lot of good a bunch of dead statues will do me."

"You pay the cab fare," insisted Mrs. O'Hara, ignoring the blasphemy. "I'll take care of the gifts."

Mrs. Kelly shuddered and her eyes moistened.

"Shush now," Mrs. O'Hara whispered, checking to see if other people noticed. "For the love of Mary. It's hard times at our end of the block, too," she said, stifling tears about to run her mascara.

"You're a kind woman. I didn't mean to be so rude," Mrs. Kelly murmured. "And after the baby comes," she wiped her eyes, "I'll knit the little bugger something wonderful."

"That would be heavenly."

"If you don't mind me sayin' so, I don't know much 'bout heaven." Mrs. Kelly sniffled. "But enough of this, this chatter. Let's get shopping so we can spend as much time as possible with Katherine." Her voice darkened. "I gotta be home before four o'clock."

The women rummaged through piles of cotton blankets. They selected a blue print featuring baby robins nuzzled in a nest, their mother on a sprig looking on as they slept. The bib was an obvious choice – blue with a cow jumping over the moon. Mrs. O'Hara tossed a rattle and pacifier into the bag, as well as a tiny valise.

"You never know," she commented, "Ron, Katherine and the baby might take a vacation."

Mrs. Kelly arched her eyebrows, a silent scoff.

"Now here's somethin' practical," she said, plucking a diaper bag from a heap of clearance items. "Do you remember what it was like to get rid of diapers when you were out in public?"

The stink and frenzy familiar to all first-time mothers returned to Mrs. O'Hara. "Yes," she said. "You'd better put that thing in the bag." She calculated the total cost of the items. "Close to fifteen dollars. I've got about ten more to go."

They walked to the maternity racks. On display were many styles and colors.

"She's in her third trimester, right," asked Mrs. Kelly.

"Yes. The baby's due around Christmas."

Third trimester clothing was at the far end. Once there, each woman took turns holding tops to bottoms in order to determine which would be the best selection for Katherine.

"What do ya think," asked Mrs. Kelly. She held up a bright orange top and black pants.

"I like the bottoms," replied Mrs. O'Hara. "Black goes with anything, but the orange, eh." She spotted another shirt. "Here, hold this up."

Mrs. Kelly reluctantly switched the orange with the green.

"Now, I like that," remarked Mrs. O'Hara. "What do you think?" She took the outfit and held it to her plump figure.

"Green? Really? Well, she's your daughter."

Mrs. O'Hara offered a thin smile as she removed the items from the hangers and put them in the bag.

"That's it," she said, "almost twenty dollars." She ran her finger through her hair. "You know, we'll use the change to buy something sweet when we get to the Cloverleaf."

"That sounds great."

At the far end of the store, a large Roman numeral wall clock struck two. After the gong faded Mrs. O'Hara said, "Where has the time gone? We'd better get a move on."

"I know," said Mrs. Kelly. "We gotta hurry up and find a place to pay."

In the maternity section, a line of customers waited for slow-moving cashiers. Mrs. Kelly searched for alternative checkout stations, hand to her forehead.

"Over there, in the toy department," she whispered, not wanting to alert other shoppers. "There's a cashier doing nothing but touching up her lipstick."

As the out-of-place women approached, the cashier looked down her nose.

"Did you find everything you needed, ladies?"

Mrs. O'Hara removed each item from the shopping bag. "Yes. I did."

Mrs. Kelly took notice of the time again.

The cashier methodically clipped price tags and slowly punched keys on the register. "That'll be nineteen dollars and seventy-two cents," she said. "Cash, check or Jordan's charge?"

"Cash," replied Mrs. O'Hara as she reached into her purse and dropped the wad of fives on the counter. The cashier stared at the crumpled money.

"Excuse me," said Mrs. O'Hara. She removed one of the bills, returned it to her purse and ironed the others with her palm.

"Would you like any of your items gift wrapped," asked the bemused cashier.

"No, we haven't time," Mrs. Kelly interrupted.

"Very well." She folded white tissue paper around the outfit and gently placed it in the fancy shopping bag along with the tiny valise. Rattles and other items were put into the diaper bag. "Thank you for shopping Jordan's," she added.

The women walked toward the elevators. As Mrs. O'Hara paused to rub her sore feet, Mrs. Kelly turned around just in time to catch the clock strike 2:15.

"Son of a bitch," she whispered.

"What'd you say?" said Mrs. O'Hara

"Nothing. Just thinking about the cute booties."

The shopping crowd had thinned. The elevator operator, snacking on peanuts, gave the women an express ride.

"Goo' day, ladies," he said with a tip of his cap.

The women hurried to the store's exit. Gold doors swung outward. "Thank you for shopping Jordan's." The Beefeater bowed.

"I could get used to this," Mrs. O'Hara gushed.

"Yeah, it's somethin'," replied Mrs. Kelly. "Lets get goin'."

Out on the sidewalk, she shifted the shopping bag to her other hand. "We're in luck. There's a vacant cab." She whistled like a sailor. "Hey, cabbie. Over here."

The cab pulled to where Mrs. Kelly stood. She opened the back door.

"Hurry and get in," she said. "I'll pass the big bag to you once you're settled."

Mrs. O'Hara scooted across the back seat, diaper bag in hand.

"Where to, lady?" the driver asked.

"Cloverleaf."

"You mean the old…"

"I mean the nice diner out near the truck entrance, sir." Mrs. O'Hara adjusted her skirt.

"Okay," she said. "I'm all set. Let me have it." She extended her hand. The shopping bag was thrown into the back of the cab. It almost struck her in the face. Startled, she looked to her right. A bloated figure stood outside the open door. Bob Kelly raised one fist, the other hand clamped on his wife's forearm.

Mrs. O'Hara now saw nothing but his pitch eyes.

"A little birdy told me ya was gonna be here with my wife. I'll let ya have it, ya Catholic scum," he murmured as he reached into the cab, his arm cocked.

She froze.

No escape.

The driver looked in the rearview mirror.

"Hey, buddy," he warned. "I don't give a good goddamn what you and your old lady do in your own place, but none of that shit in my cab." He made a point of holding a nightstick high enough for Mr. Kelly's benefit.

Kelly lowered his fist. "Listen bitch and listen good," he whispered. "Ya screwed with my family for the last time. Tell that to ya whore daughter and scumbag husband."

Mrs. O'Hara unfroze and glanced out the window. Mrs. Kelly's happiness had shriveled, her head sunk to her shoulders. A look of surrender swept over her, just waiting for the end. Bob Kelly threatened with his fist before slamming the door.

"We still goin' to that *diner*, lady?" the driver said.

Mrs. O'Hara stared out the rear window as Mr. Kelly dragged his wife off. People on the street paid little attention. No one seemed to care. And before dwindling into the crowd, Mrs. Kelly looked over her shoulder and offered a meek wave goodbye.

"Hey, lady," the driver said, now annoyed.

She didn't react.

"I said, *lady*! Are we goin' or not?"

Other cabs tooted impatience.

"Yes. We are going."

"Okay, then." He popped the clutch and pulled away.

35.

"Look! Look at what you've done to me!" Katherine screamed to her naked reflection, turning a profile in the bathroom mirror, left then right. "Disgusting pig!" Sobs filled the cabin, her face buried in her hands. "I should've gotten rid of you from the start."

She balled her fists, ready to pummel the hell out of her mid-section. As she raised her arms, prepared to thrust downward, something stopped her. She raised her arms a second time. No use.

"I can't do it." She flopped on the toilet seat.

"Hey. What's goin' on in there?" Geary pounded the cabin door.

"What do you want? I told you. I'm not working."

"This isn't about work."

Silence.

"Katherine," Geary's voice softened to a purr, "will you open the door? Please?"

She tiptoed to the front window and looked through the blinds.

"Oh, Jesus!" She trotted back to the bathroom. "Gimme a minute, will you?"

A bed sheet with three holes hung from the door hook. She put her head through the large hole and her arms through two smaller openings. She wrapped a piece of clothesline around her waist and answered the door.

"Mother. What on earth are you doing here? You should've let me know you were coming."

Mrs. O'Hara's expression said it all. Let me in!

" I, I wasn't expecting…" Katherine continued.

Geary pushed open the door enough for Mrs. O'Hara to enter. She surveyed the cabin with disgust. Greasy dishes, take-out boxes and moldy leftovers littered the kitchenette. Ron's dirty clothes were in a heap near the bed. Maternity outfits – gifts from the clothing drive – were strewn throughout the two hundred square foot cabin. Her daughter's appearance stole her breath.

"What are you? Some, some kind of roadside gypsy?"

Katherine stepped back. "It's been so busy with Ron studying and all. I haven't had time to clean."

The Jordan's shopping bag slipped from Mrs. O Hara's hand. She placed the diaper bag next to it. Geary stood behind her.

"Mr. Geary," she apologized, "please don't take offense to what I just said."

"None taken." His eyes met Katherine's. "I gotta get back to the diner." He left, closing the door behind him.

Mrs. O'Hara waited until Geary was out of earshot. She turned to Katherine and snarled, "Your father told me this place was unkempt, but this, this is a pigsty." Starting in the kitchenette, she began a massive cleanup. "Don't just stand there," she said, "get out of that, whatever it is, and put on the outfit in the shopping bag then get yourself over here and help me."

Katherine shuffled barefoot to the Jordan's bag. "I wouldn't be caught dead in any of that used junk the church sends over."

"Oh, is that why you prance around in something that displays the shadow of your privates? Have you no shame?"

"I have plenty…." Katherine began, but her mother cut her off.

"I'm wearing some of that 'junk', as you call it," Mrs. O' Hara said. "You don't think I know some other woman cast it off as trash?"

With fingers clamped to her nostrils, she plucked a rotten tomato from the counter and searched for something to use as a waste container. Katherine moved a pile of dirty underwear and sat on the edge of the bed.

"Mother," she sulked, "I want to kill myself."

The tomato fell to the floor with a damp thud. She rushed to her daughter's side.

"What in God's name are you saying, girl," her voice grave but hushed. "You know it's a *mortal* sin, a *mortal* sin. You'd be guilty of *two* murders. Yours and the beautiful child you're carrying. Hell would be your home for eternity." She paused a moment to quell her temper. "The Lord gives each of us our own cross to bear and it's our job to make the best of what He has provided. He and He alone calls us home."

"It would be better to be dead in hell than alive," Katherine screamed. "That's where I am now." She bolted to her feet. "I'm in goddamn hell on earth!"

Mrs. O'Hara didn't have enough hands, wanting to cover her eyes and ears.

"Oh, Katherine. I don't know you anymore. What's gone so wrong that'd cause you to say such things and to, to take the Lord's name in vain? To talk of suicide?"

"This!" she shouted, poking her stomach. "This is what's wrong!"

"Honey." Her mother sat on the bed and patted the soiled sheet, suggesting Katherine join her. "Sweetheart. It's not the end of the world. I know you feel like you'll never be young again. Like there's nothing but drudgery and responsibility ahead." She stroked Katherine's hair. "All young mothers think that." Her finger gently touched

Katherine's chin so their eyes might meet. "You'll have fun again. I promise. Your father and me, we'll want to spend so much time with that kid, you'll think it's ours. You and Ron will have plenty of time to enjoy your youth."

"Seriously?" Katherine's angry eyes softened.

"Seriously," she said as Katherine rested her head on her shoulder. A minute passed then Mrs. O'Hara stood and brought Katherine to her feet at the same time. "I came here today because I wanted to surprise you with a baby shower." She passed the Jordan's bag and diaper carrier.

"You mean these things aren't from the church? You went to Jordan's?"

"No. They're not from the church and yes I went to Jordan's. Why don't you try on the outfit and I'll start cleaning."

"Mother," Katherine whispered, "where'd you get the money?"

"It's not important."

"Mother?"

"Yes?"

"I'm sorry. I didn't mean 'kill' myself. I just feel dead sometimes. I'm so ashamed." She closed her eyes.

"You never have to be ashamed, sweetheart. I'm your mother. We don't keep secrets."

Katherine kissed her cheek and went into the bathroom, gently closing the door.

Mrs. O'Hara gave a heavy sigh. "I have to do something about these darn shoes." She considered going barefoot, but caked road dirt and a mysterious dried liquid on the linoleum convinced her otherwise. Instead, she folded sections from a recent copy of the *Hearth* until there were four little pads, a set for the tops of her battered toes and two that wrapped around her raw heels. She tucked them inside her shoes. "Ah, at least I can move."

Enough paper remained to dispose of the old food – a green, roast beef sandwich. She wrapped it in the *Local Section.* The last fold revealed the headline:

**RABBLE-ROUSING NEGRO HAS
THREE MORE WEEKS**

The story recapped Archie's murder and Ben's involvement. As she read, she fought the urge to faint. The thought of what had happened in front of Jordan's brought a rush of anxiety. Her underarms dripped. The strength went out of her. She began to go down, but grabbed the kitchen counter just in time as the bathroom door swung open.

"Katherine. You look darling."

36.

Mrs. O'Hara and her aching feet dragged up the front steps and into the house, thankful to be home ahead of her husband. Drained by the day's drama, she painfully stepped out of the oversize shoes, removed the charity outfit and shoved her arms into a gray quilted housecoat. She covered the ten feet to the kitchen, her tattered slippers scuffing the floor like sandpaper.

What can I put together in a hurry?

A search of the refrigerator presented one option, thawed butler steak. She twisted the gas jet to half, dropped a slab of butter in the skillet and watched it melt. In went the meat. She boiled a pot of water and added frozen peas and carrots

"Smells good," her husband shouted, gently closing the front door. As usual, he hung his gun belt on the hook, his cap next to it. "How's my beauty," he called from the hallway.

"Wash up, John. I'll have supper ready in a few."

The old steps creaked under his weight. The bathroom door shut and taps screeched as water flowed. He hummed a happy melody – some old Irish folk tune.

Bob Kelly's bloated face hung in her mind. Five minutes went by. The unattended meat swam in burnt butter, while boiled vegetables overflowed onto the stovetop.

"Elizabeth? What're you doing?" Mr. O'Hara rushed into the kitchen and shut down the gas. With that, Kelly's image disappeared from her mind.

"Oh, I'm sorry." Her hands fluttered, unsure of their next move. She looked around the room until her eyes met his. She buried her face in his chest. "Here, what's all this," he asked, stroking the back of her head.

He eased her face from his shirt.

"Sit," she sniffled, "let me make you a plate."

"Are you okay?"

"Yes. I'm fine. It's just that I saw Katherine today."

"How'd you get all the way out there?"

Mrs. O'Hara pretended not to hear the question.

He sat in his favorite wooden chair, took hold of its armrests and slid close to the kitchen table. She put a plate of food down and sat across from him.

"Sorry," she reiterated as he chewed on the overcooked meat. "It was the only thing I could throw together before you got home."

He wagged a finger, "No, dear," a hard swallow, "it's fine. Just fine." He cut another piece of steak. "How'd you get out there," he repeated putting another chunk in his reluctant mouth, working it from side to side.

"I went to town with Mrs. Kelly."

A lump of burnt fat lodged midway in Mr. O'Hara's throat. In a panic, he worked his neck muscles until it cleared.

"Elizabeth," he said between gasps. "What on earth are you doing," a hacking cough, "with, with that woman?"

Her fingernails dug into the housecoat, almost breaking skin on her kneecaps. Her head bowed and two words followed.

"Bob Kelly."

"What about Bob Kelly," he asked, tilting her chin upward.

"I wanted to surprise Katherine with a baby shower. You know, something we girls do. Mrs. Kelly was the only person I could think of who had a right to be there." She paused to breathe. "She'll be grandmother to the child, you know. Anyway. We, we went downtown to get a few small gifts." Tears dropped to the table. "When we finished, Mrs. Kelly hailed a taxi and I got in." She covered her eyes with her palms. "It was horrible."

"What? What was horrible?"

"I got in the cab and when I turned to take the packages from Mrs. Kelly, Bob Kelly threw them at me. He came out of nowhere and he said things. Bad things. John, I'm scared."

Mr. O'Hara went to her side, embraced her and whispered in her ear. "There's no need to be frightened, Elizabeth. I'm here. Now, what did he say?"

She stared at the kitchen wall, her eyes round and wet. "He called me Catholic scum, you a coward and Katherine a whore."

O'Hara raised his fist, about to slam the table, but stopped mid-swing.

"Did the man have anything else to say?"

"Yes," she gulped. "He said it was the last time we'd interfere with his family."

"Did he *touch* you, Elizabeth?"

"I, I think he was going to hit me, but the cabdriver pulled a Paddy whacker and that stopped him."

O'Hara held his breath, his teeth grinding.

She stood and twirled once around. "Don't do anything. I'm all right. I'm okay. Look! It's Mrs. Kelly I fear for. I don't know what that monster will do to her."

He paced the floor, looking toward the hallway and the gun hanging on the hook.

37.

O'Hara pledged to the missus with breathless intimacy that he would do or say nothing to Bob Kelly if their paths crossed. After a kiss, it was off to work.

Upon his arrival, the night guards cheered, "Marty's Tavern. And away we go," imitating the popular TV star Jackie Gleason and his famous exits from the stage.

In the meantime, three young day-shift guards greeted O'Hara with a salute. He scratched his forehead. They took the gesture as a return salute then went to their positions, waiting for workers to arrive.

O'Hara snatched a copy of the *Hearth* from one of the youngsters. He flipped the pages while on the way to spend the day in an old house trailer that should've been hauled off after the invention of indoor plumbing.

He yawned, planted his butt in a wooden chair near the soot-stained window, and buried his face in the newspaper. Once in a while, he peered over the top to check things out. The procession of workers came and went. The young guards examined badges and occasionally searched a lunchbox.

After the 8:00 a.m. whistle, assured he wouldn't bump into Kelly or anybody else he didn't want to see, he got up to visit the latrine, a boxed-shaped, sheet metal structure on the other side of the guardhouse, just outside the gate.

A smudged light bulb in an overhead socket lit the space no more than dusk or dawn. When finished, he dipped his fingers in soapy water. At that moment the latrine door squeaked. Daylight shot in.

"Mornin'," he offered though he couldn't see the person as he glanced over his shoulder.

"Yeah, fuck off," replied the figure walking through the doorway.

Hung-over asshole, O'Hara thought, wiping his hands with a swatch of damp terrycloth.

The man took a seat in the far stall. O'Hara listened. Who the hell is that, he wondered.

After a throaty hack, the man moaned, "I had to crap a Catholic mile."

It's Kelly. I should go in there while his pants are down and stuff his head in the toilet.

O'Hara padded to the stall. Kelly shouted, "What? Ya lookin' for a cheap thrill, faggot?"

O'Hara raised his foot, about to drive it through the stall door and send Kelly down the tubes with the rest of his waste, but stopped.

John, promise you won't get involved with that monster.

O'Hara darted from the putrid hut. As he passed the checkpoint nearest the trailer, he ducked in, asking a young, athletic-looking cop, "Hey, son. Do me a favor, will you?"

"Anything you want, sir," the freckled-faced guard replied.

"There's a fat turd in the latrine. When he comes out, call him over and check his lunch box. You might find a pint of contraband."

The kid's eyes lit up. "You think I can get my first bust, sir?"

"You never know what you'll reel in when you fish the swamp, son."

The kid rocked his head side to side. "I'll handle it, Officer O'Hara. You can count on me."

"Ah. That's a good lad."

O'Hara retreated to his trailer and opened the window to listen, still using the newspaper as cover. Enough time elapsed that he began to read a story. As he wet his thumb to turn the page the young guard hollered, "Hey, you. Yeah. You! This way."

O'Hara peeked and saw the kid motioning to Kelly, who froze with his hands on his hips. "Who you talkin' to," Kelly said.

Once more, the young guard beckoned. Kelly swiveled his head, and shot a lump of mucus the size of a toad to the ground then complied.

O'Hara smiled. Oh, this will be a good one, he thought.

The guard held his hand out. Kelly smacked the metal ID badge into the kid's palm, expecting a painful reaction. The guard stood expressionless.

"Okay, sir," he said. "Now that you've had your exercise for the day, let's see the lunchbox." He didn't wait for Kelly to comply. "Oh. What do we have here," he said, turning toward the trailer.

O'Hara sat silent, peeking around the paper as the youngster did his job.

The kid fished out a sandwich wrapped in wax paper, a Thermos (which he opened and sniffed) and a ten-inch buck knife, deerskin handle and all.

Kelly seethed.

A smile grew on O'Hara's face.

"This blade's over six inches. Sorry, no weapons allowed on the job." The guard placed the knife on the counter. Kelly tried to grab it, but the kid snatched it away.

"It'll be here waiting when you're done with your shift."

He passed the lunchbox to Kelly, motioning with his eyes to the clock and his thumb toward the dock, for Kelly to get to work.

Incensed, the crane operator took his badge and lunch pail. Before continuing past the gate, he glowered toward the trailer. "I know ya in there, ya coward," he yelled. "I'm not done with ya. I'm not done. Ya hear me?"

O'Hara dropped the paper, exposing his face. "God damn you, you worthless piece of humanity," his body a sea of trembles as he hollered back. "I hope a load of coke drops on your head. Just like you did to that poor colored boy."

"I don't know what ya're talkin' about."

O'Hara moved to the trailer steps. The young guard joined him as they watched Kelly lumber toward the dock.

"What happened to make that guy so angry," the kid asked.

"Nothing that hasn't happened to any of us. He's just bad, son," O'Hara said. "There's no one to blame. He's hateful. Period."

O'Hara patted the kid's back. "You did good today, young man. I'll make sure Captain Sullivan gets word."

"Thanks, Officer O'Hara." The kid turned to leave.

"Son. Wait a second, will you?"

"Sure, sir. What can I do for you?"

O'Hara's shoes scraped the gravel. "Why do you lads salute me? I'm no higher in rank than you."

With a smile the kid replied, "It's nothing to do with rank. It's respect." Now the kid shuffled his feet. "You see, Officer O'Hara, we know what you've been through and…one mistake doesn't make a man. We respect you."

Heat came to O'Hara's face. His eyes welled. "I see." He coughed. "Well, well, that is something now, isn't it?" He rested his hand on the young man's shoulder. "You're a good bunch, you are."

The kid gave a crisp salute and marched to his position. O'Hara trembled as he entered the dingy trailer. He had just committed mortal sin: wishing death on another human being and taking the Lord's name in vain. In his mind, both acts guaranteed him a front row seat on the express ride to hell. His pale skin went cold. His sweaty face drew near a wall mirror veined with cracks. He studied his distorted image. "Please, Jesus, forgive me," he asked.

38.

That same morning, a few hours earlier, Ron languished in bed. He stared out the cabin window, observing the pinks and blues of dawn as they overtook the silver moonlight. A limp Lucky hung from his yellowed fingers. He blew a final round of smoke rings, which expanded into nothingness. As he reached for an ashtray, Katherine stirred.

"What time is it?" she groaned.

"Go back to sleep, baby. It's early," he whispered, crushing the butt.

She wiped sleep from her eye, ran her hands over her bloated belly and struggled to her side. "The little sucker is trying to kick his way out," she said, pulling Ron's hand to her mid-section. He tenderly touched her stomach. He felt it bounce.

"Is that normal," he murmured. "That baby's acting like it wants to break loose."

"The doctor told me that kicking varies. Some babies are quiet as a church mouse while others act like they're making a jailbreak." She quickly changed subjects. "Are you ready for the test today?"

He let out a long sigh. "As ready as I'll ever be." His hand covered his eyes.

"What's wrong, Ron? You are ready, aren't you?"

"I'm more than ready."

"Then what's eating you?"

He swung his legs over the edge of the bed, feet to the chilly floor.

"I feel like I don't deserve any of this. You, the baby, and Geary helping us. Your mom and dad tried to put some order in our screwed-up lives. But my family's done nothing."

Katherine wiggled up the headboard, her belly supported with one hand.

"I thought guilt was reserved for Catholics," she scoffed.

"Don't be cute." He wiped spittle from the corner of his mouth. "You remember Isaac, don't you?"

Katherine showed no emotion. "Yes."

"Well, so do I and he's rotting to shit up there in a potter's grave because he was *black* and he dared to help *us.*"

Ron paused and lit another cigarette.

"The whole situation sucks. Isaac's old man's been railroaded to the lock-up while his poor mother runs their store. Where's justice in this goddamn town? Tell me. Where?"

His voice boomed beyond the cabin walls. "Isaac should be taking this test, too. I know it was my old man. That bastard had something to do with Isaac's death."

He sprung from bed, his fist punching the smoky air. "Someday, I'll pay him back!"

Katherine barrel-rolled out of bed and yanked his quaking arm.

"Don't do anything stupid, Ron. He's not worth it." Her intensity trumped his anger. "You're about to be a father," she reminded him. "And when you pass your test we're going to have a new life away from all of this. Some place where people treat one another with respect. Some place peaceful where we can start over, where nobody knows us." She waved her arm like it was a magic wand.

Leave Battle Hymn altogether? It had never occurred to Ron.

"Maybe you're right," he said. "When I pass the test, we'll move outta this place. It'll be the three of us, you, me and the baby. As long as we're together, that's all that matters.

39.

Ron and Katherine stepped into a fist of cold air. "Look," she pointed, her voice sleepy. "It's only October and I can see my breath." Her childlike fascination derailed him from worrying about the test.

"You're beautiful," Ron whispered and pecked her forehead.

"I'm hungry as hell, that's what I am," she said.

When they came to the front of the diner, engine rumbles grew louder. A convoy of ten flatbeds loaded with rolls of steel cable idled while puffs of black exhaust tinted the air.

"The place is busy. I hope Geary has time to make us something hot," Ron said

Inside the diner, silverware banged dishes and truckers conversed through mouthfuls of food. Both were accented by occasional demands for more coffee and "hey, bring us a check." Ron and Katherine flopped in their usual spot.

Though she wore the new outfit her mother had purchased, long gone were the days of truck drivers ogling. Pregnancy had robbed her of her angelic features. Pimples dotted her face. Her green eyes were now victims of perpetual fatigue.

Geary hustled from the kitchen.

"Big day," he said, sliding two breakfast specials across the table. One plate stopped in front of Katherine. Ron caught the other just before eggs, bacon and biscuits dropped in his lap.

"Nice catch," Geary grinned. "I overshot the runway."

"No problem," Ron replied. "Yeah, it's a big day." He chewed on a piece of bacon.

Geary knelt to look Katherine in the eye.

"What's wrong," he asked.

"I'm fine. Just a little tired." She winced and held her stomach, fighting the urge to groan. "Gas," she lied.

Ron concentrated on breakfast and looking out the window.

"Oh shit. My ride's here."

Lenny pulled the milk van into a space reserved for deliveries and tooted the horn.

That signaled there wouldn't be anything for the diner that morning. A biscuit and one slice of bacon whirled in Ron's mouth. He scooted from the booth, turned and blew Katherine a sloppy kiss.

"I'll see you tonight," she replied.

Geary stood, taking Ron's hand in his stone hard grip. "Today's gonna change everything for the two – I mean three – of you," he laughed.

"We know," said Ron. "Things will be different for all of us. Katherine and me, we'll be out of your hair." He squeezed Geary's hand as hard as possible. "If it weren't for you, Joe, I don't know what would have happened to us."

"I know a good bet when I see one," Geary said. He regarded his booming business. "You two were a sure thing."

Lenny gave another toot.

"I guess he's in a hurry," Katherine said. "You'd better get going." She winced again.

"You okay," Ron asked.

"Kid, didn't you hear a word I said to her," Geary asked.

Katherine cut them off. "I'll be fine if I can get some food in me," she said. "Now git outta here and go pass that test."

"Pregnant girls! Gees! Happy one minute, a ball of fire the next," Ron joked. After a final slug of coffee, he said, "I'll see you tonight, baby."

With Ron and Lenny out of the picture, Geary sidled up to Katherine. "You sure you're all right?"

She took a bite of a butter biscuit.

"Yeah. Yeah. I'm fine. I told you. Just a little gas."

Not convinced, Geary said, "You can't fool me."

She swallowed. "I know," then rested her hand on the massive bicep bulging underneath his tee shirt. "If I have any problems, I'll come get you."

"Okay. But promise me." He scanned his busy diner. "Things can happen fast during the last three months of pregnancy."

Katherine stared at her plate.

"I know," she said.

As he headed toward the kitchen, a trucker, his face buried in breakfast, dangled a coffee mug from his thumb and yelled, "Hey, will one of you dumb-asses get me a refill?"

Geary went to the table. He extended his hand, palm up. "Ahem," he coughed.

The driver looked up, prepared to supply an additional wisecrack. His sneer went flat. He handed the cup to Geary.

"Please?"

"That's more like it, buddy. I'll be right back." Before he went to get the refill, he stopped at Katherine's table again. "Listen, young lady, I want to come by the cabin and check on you."

She had finished her food and scavenged Ron's crumbs. "You don't have to do that," she said.

"Humor me?"

"Well, if you insist. But I told you, I'm fine."

When she got back to the cabin she peeled off the store-bought maternity outfit and returned to the makeshift toga. Due to her mother's hard work, the place was clean and orderly, but Katherine still felt like she lived in a hole. During a pee, ripples of pain hit her head-to-toe.

"Ah! This horrible thing!" She flushed the toilet, drew the blinds and got into bed. "God! This is your fault."

A wave of fatigue rushed through her. She rolled to her side and slept. There was nothing at first, but soon, her dreams became a dangerous place. Twitches and a jerk here and there thrust her back into a day she had struggled to forget.

No. No. No. Her body quivered. *Not this. It's a sin, but I can't fight you. God help me."*

* * *

Back on Wood Street, Mrs. Kelly convalesced on the front porch. Her husband's beat down after the encounter at Jordan's had left no visible bruises. He'd kept it simple; a rag around the neck, a foot to the back and a few head dunks in the toilet.

Sitting out in public wasn't her first choice, but no matter where she stood, sat or lay, the house was too cold. She didn't care if she ever went inside again.

Old Lady Magee, wearing a told-you-so puss, watered her ragged mums on the other side of the rail. Mrs. Kelly watched the plant-to-plant shuffle. *It was you, wasn't it? You told him I was with Mrs. O'Hara. I could kill you.* Magee glanced with a look that suggested she might be a mind reader.

"The Cold weather's coming early this year. Don't you think, Mrs. Magee?"

"It's October, what do you expect?" she replied.
Mrs. Kelly folded her hands and stared at the street.
How can I leave? Where will I go?

40.

Several hours before his mother debated her exodus, Ron wheeled the last pallet of milk to the commissary walk-in. Lenny not far behind, teased, "So you're gonna be a big-time electrician."

"Not at first," said Ron. "It's a step at a time. I'll start out as an apprentice. A few years later I'll be a journeyman." A rush of chilled air hit him when he opened the cooler's door.

Lenny pitched in to stack gallon containers and pints of milk.

"You gonna stay at the mill or go off on your own," he asked.

"Katherine's been talking about moving away from here, but I don't think that's gonna happen. This mill's all I know." Ron paused. "I guess it's all I'll ever know."

Lenny looked at his watch. "Son, I've enjoyed your company these past few months. I'm not embarrassed to tell you." He gave a little laugh. "It gets a little lonely shuttling things from one cooler to the other." He slipped the white cap from his head. "Heck," he continued. "It wasn't until Geary cleaned up that old brothel that I saw people on a regular basis."

"How many years you been doin' this," Ron asked.

Lenny counted his fingers, looked at his feet, still counting, then to the ceiling. "Twenty-eight, next month. Twenty-eight years."

Ron continued to unload and stack milk containers. "That's a long time."

"It has good points, son. Don't get me wrong. In the early morning most of the world's sleepy and friendly." Lenny slapped the hat back on his head. "In the beginning," he chuckled, "I had a wagon with two wonderful mules. They were my company until the van came along." He stacked the last of the fifty milk containers. "I sure miss Ezra and Amos. That's what I called them, anyway. They were good mules."

Ron wheeled the empty milk cart back to the truck. Lenny extended his weathered hand. "Well, I guess this is it," he said.

"What," Ron replied, perplexed.

"You won't be needin' me anymore. You'll be gettin your own place and all."

"Whoa." Ron held his hands up. "It's gonna take a while. Katherine and me, we'll be at Geary's until the baby comes. That's in December."

"Oh." Lenny's brow relaxed. "I guess I got ahead of myself. I thought you'd be outta here right after you took that test."

Ron collected his study material from the front seat. "Nah, Len," he said. "You'll have to put up with me for a few more months."

"That'd be just fine."

"Gotta run, buddy." Ron patted the old milkman's shoulder. "Whistle's gonna blow."

He jumped from the loading dock to the driveway and sprinted toward corporate headquarters.

"Good luck. You're nicest white kid I ever knew," Lenny called to the boy's fading image.

41.

By noon, Kelly had almost crapped his pants. "Too much booze," he shouted. If not for the screech of the crane, the entire dock would have heard about his bowel disorder.

"Ah shit," he moaned and shut down the machine. Once on terra firma, he told Duffy that the Dublin bar was where the world could find him. It was an uncomfortable walk to the security gate, but he collected his buck-knife from the guard, made a stop at the latrine and continued onward.

O'Hara had just missed him. He was in the main building. Captain Sullivan wanted someone to talk to during a mid-day meal of beets and hardboiled eggs.

* * *

Not far from Sullivan's office, Ron was halfway through the test. After lunch, he would have to complete a mock-up of a boiler room electrical panel. No sweat, he thought, the tough stuff's behind me. In the commissary, he watched low-level executives, secretaries and spit-shined maintenance workers snatching milk containers he had unloaded hours earlier. Seated at a corner table, he pondered Katherine's suggestion: *We'll move away from here where nobody knows us.*

* * *

Geary pumped out food orders wishing the lull of summer was upon his business instead of autumn's constant sprint. A rare moment of equilibrium between hungry customers, the kitchen and the register gave him a minute to notice the time. He slid a burger and fries through the pick-up window.

"Jones," he shouted to his grill man. "I'll be back. I've gotta check on something."

Before knocking, he put his ear to the door of cabin six. After hearing moans and "Christ, help me," he burst in to find Katherine on the edge of the bed, body drenched in sweat, both hands supporting her stomach.

She whimpered, "Help."

He eased her onto her back. "Stay calm, young lady. I'll be right with you."

Three giant strides later, he retrieved the keys to Jones' car, a wood-paneled Ford station wagon with huge Air Force decals plastered on its tailgate.

Geary backed the decorated car to the door. He dashed to cabin number five and removed the clean bedding. After spreading the sheets and a blanket on the passenger seat, he tossed a pillow in and returned to Katherine, who shifted side-to-side, as bolts of labor grew more frequent.

"Okay, honey. We're going to Battle Hymn General. Who's your doctor?"

Katherine pointed to the kitchenette.

"There on the counter," she groaned. "His card's there."

"I'm gonna put you in the car, then," he studied the small print, "I'll give Dr. White a call to let him know we're on the way."

"Ahhh, Christ," she screamed as another wave hit.

Geary tenderly laid her on the thick bedding then threw a dime in a nearby payphone. After five rings and a brief search by an orderly, Dr. White came to the receiver.

"Doc, I'm bringin' in one of your patients. What's her name? Katherine O'Hara. She's in labor. You were expectin' it? Okay, we're on our way."

At first, he drove slowly. But on the highway he asked the old car for all it had. Katherine screeched, groaned then fell silent.

Geary thought, should I deliver the baby myself?

He pulled to the side of the road. She screamed bloody murder. Premature babies are a handful, he recalled as he swung his free arm over and stroked her forehead.

"It's okay, Katherine. We'll be at the hospital in a few minutes."

He dodged traffic, looking to Katherine from time to time.

"Joe," she grunted. "Do you think I'm pretty?"

"What are you talking about? Sure I do." He looked to the road and touched her cheek.

"Why don't you have someone to care for you," she asked.

"I had someone," he said, "the most important and wonderful person I'd ever met."

"What happened?"

"A few years back, while delivering medicine, a chopper crashed. Fate stole him from me."

"Him?" she asked, almost forgetting her pain. "Is that why you told my father kids and a wife weren't in the cards for you? You're queer?"

"Not queer, kid. Just a guy who was in love."

"I can't believe it," she chortled.

"Believe what?"

Her grunts combined with laughter. "Arrr, this hurts."

"Believe what," Geary repeated.

Her laughter flickered brightly then faded.

"And I thought I had a big secret," she said. "You'll be going to hell faster than me."

"Hell? Well, ain't that just great," he sighed. "Is there anything you want me to tell the devil when I get there?"

"Yeah. If I'm not already sitting on his lap, tell him I'm right behind you."

He put both hands on the wheel. "Listen. Despite what those penguins taught you in Catholic school, hell's where you make it, honey."

"Why did you come to Battle Hymn in the first place?"

Geary swallowed his anger. "You wanna know why I came here?"

She didn't respond.

"I came here because after I lost the love of my life, I felt like the world was a tub of shit. Instead of sittin' 'round feeling sorry for myself, I quit the Corps and decided to dive in and start at the bottom by turning a trucker whorehouse into a nice restaurant and a clean motel."

Katherine closed her eyes and absorbed another jolt as she pondered Geary's words "feel sorry for myself." At that moment her water broke and drenched the bedding.

The car came to a jerky stop under the emergency room's canopy. Geary met the orderlies and helped Katherine onto a gurney.

Before she was whisked to maternity he said, "I've gotta get back to the diner. And you listen up. I don't know what you're hiding, but don't let it rule you. You're about to take on life's biggest role."

"To hell with all men!" she screamed.

Geary shook his head. "Poor kid," he said. "You'll see it different in the morning." As they wheeled her away, he snapped his finger. *I'd better get hold of Ron.*

He jumped in the car. A few minutes later, he was turned away at the mill's truck entrance. "I can't let you pass without an ID badge," the guard said.

"Can you at least get a message to somebody," Geary begged.

"What's his name?"

"Ron Kelly. He's takin' a test in the main building. Tell him his wife's in the hospital."

"Kelly?" The guard scratched his chin. "I'll see what I can do."

Just then, an air horn blasted. "Get this jalopy outta the way," the guard commanded. "I've got deliveries coming."

Geary stuck his arm out the window, his finger taking dead aim at the guard's throat.

"Promise me you'll call."

The guard got the message.

"I'll call as soon as I check this truck in. I promise."

Satisfied, Geary made a U-turn and headed back to the Cloverleaf.

* * *

Ron held two feeder cables, deciding which of the python-size wires should be attached to the electrical panel. The chubby test proctor sat on a nearby radiator, warming his butt with the season's first blast of steam heat.

An attractive young woman dressed in a smart business suit entered the room. She went to the proctor and whispered in his ear. Mission complete, she left, leaving the proctor to rub his face as he walked over to where Ron stood.

Ron was deep in thought, aware of the possible fatal outcome of choosing the wrong wire.

"Hey, kid."

Startled by the interruption, Ron dropped the cable. "Am I doin' somethin' wrong," he said, bending to retrieve the wire.

"Put that down. You're done for the day."

Now fearful that he had committed an act that disqualified him from finishing the test, his arms hung limp.

"Done for the day? Whaddya mean?"

"You got a wife named Katherine?"

"What about her?"

"You can take the second half of the test next week," he said. "Your wife's over at Battle Hymn General. A guard called it in. You'd better get your ass over there."

His eyes wide, he said, "What's wrong? Is she okay? How'd she get there?"

"Hell if I know." The proctor raised his arms. "Front office says you should get your ass over there. Now go!"

Fortunately, the corporate building was near the front gate, only a half-mile from town. He ran out the door. As he hit the main drag, a blend of car exhaust and fresh soot strangled his lungs. Acid air grabbed at his eyes. His steel-tipped boots slammed the concrete sidewalk and he thought, *Katherine, our baby!*

Battle Hymn General Hospital and its ten-story brick façade stared him down. He spun through the revolving entryway, sliding across the granite floor on his greasy boots. A stunned Candy Striper covered her eyes, afraid he would topple over the reception desk and knock her flat, but Ron checked his motion by slamming sideways into the wall.

"Maternity? Maternity? Where's maternity?"

"Who are you looking for, sir," she inquired, brushing the front of her uniform.

"O'Hara, Katherine," he said between breaths.

The aide slid her finger down the hospital's patient list. "No O'Hara here, sir."

Ron shook his head. "I meant Kelly. She's my wife, Katherine Kelly."

After another skim of the list, "Ah, here we are. Katherine Kelly. She's on the sixth floor maternity, but it looks like you missed it, Mr. Kelly."

"Missed what," he shouted, drawing the attention of two orderlies who had just entered the foyer.

"They brought her from delivery about fifteen minutes ago. She's in room six-twenty. Congratulations! You're a father."

"Father? Me?"

"Yeah, you."

It hit Ron. "Are they okay? Katherine and the baby?"

"Why on earth would there be a problem?"

"The baby's premature."

"Oh, goodness. You'll have to see the doctor about that. He's probably up on..."

She didn't get a chance to finish. Ron blew past the elevator, choosing to sprint up six flights.

42.

The stairwell exit brought Ron to the entrance of the nursery and face to face with Dr. White. Almost in a trance, the elderly physician stared into the nursery, admiring his handy work, seven shriveled infants. A few squirmed or slept while others worked gum-lined mouths. Nametags written in black crayon were pinned to the top of each bassinette. One of the infants punched the air and wailed. The doctor turned to Ron.

"I could watch this all day," he said.

Ron focused on the shadowboxing baby with the name KELLY prominently displayed above its head.

"You here for someone," Dr. White asked.

Ron gaped and replied, "Uh, uh, yeah. That's my kid there. The one with the Kelly nametag."

"Oh, he's a feisty one. Good and strong."

"A boy! A son!" Ron said. "But he's premature. Will he survive?"

"Premature? That baby's almost nine months, give or a take a few days, just as I told his mother he would be."

Ron counted backwards to April. *That's only seven months. Two months early.*

"Son, you okay?"

"I, I... Where's my wife?"

"Straight down on the left. She's lucky. The ward is full and she got the only single room we have."

"Thanks, Doc."

Ron gave White's hand a quick pump and headed to the room.

Katherine's eyes were closed when he entered. He went to her bedside and touched her hand. She looked at him and said, "He looks like you. Did you see him?"

"Yeah, I did. He has the Kelly black hair, alright," his voice tender. "How do you feel?"

"I'm okay. Just a little tired."

Ron dropped her hand. He moved a few feet from the bed.

"Katherine."

"Yeah?"

"I spoke with Dr. White and he told me something I don't get."

"Don't you wanna know how I got here and the big secret I have to tell you?"

Ron bit, hoping she was about to answer the question he didn't want to ask.

"What secret?"

"Joe Geary brought me here and he told me something you won't believe."

Seeing that the conversation was headed in the wrong direction, Ron stated, "It's nice that Joe got you here, but I gotta know something." He moved closer. "What I wanna know is why Dr. White said our kid was delivered pretty close to nine months when he wasn't due until December?"

The color drained from Katherine's face. She turned to the pillow, covering her head with her arms.

"Katherine," Ron begged. "Don't be afraid. I'm just confused about the dates. That's all."

She remained in her frozen-stiff position. He tugged at her arms until they flung apart.

"You wanna know," she screamed. "You wanna know? I'll tell you. Dr. White's right. The baby's on time."

Ron stood straight, his voice calm.

"But how can that be? We weren't married until April."
Then the unthinkable question shot from his lips. "He's not
my kid?"

"He's not yours! But he's part of your goddamn
family!"

"What the hell does that mean?" He grabbed her arm
and squeezed.

"Just like him, aren't you? Using force to get your way."

"Just like who?"

"Like your old man. The father of the little boy you just
saw."

For Ron, time stopped. His blood coursed and his heart
pounded faster and faster. He raised his fist.

"Tell me what the hell you're talking about!"

"You wanna know? You want details," she cried out.
"I'll give you details. It was back in February. I shouldn't
have ever agreed to go out with you. I knew it was wrong,
but I wanted to know what it was like to date somebody
other than a Catholic. So when you asked me to meet you
downtown at the soda fountain, I said yes."

Tears of sorrow replaced her anger.

"I walked along Wood Street," she sniffled, "We agreed
to meet downtown at eight. I was early so I thought I'd
knock on your door and see if you were there. I thought we
could walk together."

Ron bent over the bed, every word bringing a stab of
pain and robbing his breath.

"Your father answered the door. I'd never met him
before, but he asked me to come in. He said you'd be home
in a minute." The light left Katherine's eyes. "When I
walked in, he locked the door behind me." Her expression
remained blank. "He had a knife." She paused and looked
toward the window. "He said if I screamed or told anybody
that he'd kill me and my parents." She turned to Ron.

"What could I do? He raped me and it was my fault. I shouldn't have been there. He stole everything." She turned away. "I'm going to hell," she cried. "And now you have a new brother. What in God's name are we going to do?"

Ron found enough strength to ask, "Why didn't you tell somebody? Anybody?"

"I told you, your father said that he'd kill me and my family." She moaned. "I had to keep my mouth shut. What could I do?"

"And that's why you rushed to marry me?"

"At first I thought about having an abortion, but the priest told me that I'd go to prison and hell if I didn't have the baby. What are we going to do," she repeated as she grabbed for his arm. "I know it was a mistake to trick you." She coughed. "But I thought that if we were married and did it fast enough everyone would think the kid was yours." Her face fell to the pillow.

Ron bolted from the hospital room.

"No, Ron, don't," she yelled. "He's not worth it."

Before descending six flights, he turned to the nursery and now quiet infant.

"I don't care where you came from," his hot breath formed on the cool glass, "You're still my son."

43.

Duffy zipped up after depositing most of his liquid lunch in the latrine. He wobbled to the door, forgoing the soap and water. As he grabbed the handle, a ruckus ensued outside. He listened as O'Hara yelled at Ron. Their voices grew louder and Duffy sought refuge in one of the stalls. The latrine door burst open. O'Hara's voice was full throttle.

"What do you mean Katherine had the baby and he's not yours? Tell me now or I'll…"

Ron was breathing fast and his words rushed from his lips.

"It was my father!"

"Your what?"

"Do you need me to spell it out? My father raped Katherine. The kid's my brother."

O'Hara relinquished his grip.

"Why, why didn't she tell us?"

"She tried. She went to the priest in that church of yours. Know what he told her?"

Silence.

Duffy, concealed on the commode with his knees to his chest, listened carefully.

"That priest told your daughter that she had to have that baby no matter what." Ron's tone calmed. "Poor Katherine. She couldn't tell anyone because my old man said he'd kill you and Mrs. O'Hara if she opened her mouth."

O'Hara found his voice. "That no good bastard."

Ron found the door and yanked it open. O'Hara grabbed his arm.

"What are you gonna do," he asked.

"What do you think," Ron said as he headed to the dock.

* * *

Duffy waited a few minutes, making sure the coast was clear before he lowered his feet and slipped from the latrine. Outside, he squinted and looked through alcohol-blurred eyes to O'Hara's dingy trailer. All he could make out was O'Hara's silhouette, talking on the phone, moving across the window, one way then another.

Duffy hiccupped then off he went, swaying toward the Dublin bar.

That afternoon, there were few patrons. Kelly and other assorted friends clotted at the far end of the bar, not wanting to be seen through the front window in case steel mill managers strolled by after a pleasant lunch at one of the town's premier steakhouses.

The six shots of whiskey Duffy downed earlier were in full effect as he fumbled up the steps and into the bar.

"Ya turd, what are you doin' back here," Kelly shouted. "Ya supposed to be coverin' for me."

"I wa...wa...was, but I got wind of somethin'."

Kelly grunted, "What'd ya do? Stick ya head up your ass and fart?"

"Good one," one of the customers cheered. "You sure know how to set 'em up."

"Na...na...seriously. I got somethin' to tell ya," Duffy slurred.

Kelly patted the empty stool. "Come here. Have another pick-me-up. Then ya can spill your guts."

Duffy grinned and joined Kelly, quaffing a shot in a single gulp.

"Okay there, me boy. Ya had your drink. Now let's hear it."

Duffy was drunk but not stupid. He moved to Kelly's ear. "Are you sure you want me to tell you in front of the other guys?"

"Don't be an idiot. We're all friends here." Kelly raised his glass.

"Are you sure?"

"Will ya spill it, ya jackass? I don't have all day."

Everyone settled in for a good story about who fucked around with whom on the dock or how someone got away with sleeping off a hangover in some new hideaway.

"I was takin' a leak," Duffy began, "and just before I left the crapper I hear this arguin' goin' on."

"Yeah, yeah, so, someone was fightin' at the gate," Kelly dismissed. "What the fuck's new about that?"

"The voices got closer so I hid in a stall. Two guys rushed into the latrine. One of 'em was O'Hara and the other was your boy. They was talkin' about how you..."

Duffy surveyed the group once more. "Are you sure you want it said out loud?"

"Enough of your shit."

"Okay. Okay. They was arguin' how you fucked O'Hara's daughter and knocked her up. She had a baby today."

Kelly shot out of his seat, nostrils flared. No one dared interrupt this moment as he stared at the ceiling, for they all knew Bob Kelly. Finally, he broke the silence.

"Where's Katherine O Hara?"

"She's at Battle Hymn General on the sixth floor. I heard Ron say it."

"Where's my traitor son?"

"He's huntin' you."

Kelly whipped out his buck knife and ran his finger along its edge.

"First things first," he said. "I told her what would happen if she said a fuckin' word." He slipped the blade back into its sheath, pounded down a shot and left the bar.

Duffy stayed behind, deciding to have another round or two before heading back to the dock. After three glasses of whiskey, he bid farewell to Tommy the bartender and the remaining two customers.

"Good thing there's a railing on these steps," he babbled, one foot in front of the other. Once on the sidewalk, he directed his feet to walk toward the mill. There were a few false starts, but his newly christened legs got the message. He kept close to the curb. "Too many damn ped...pedes...too many people walkin'," he said.

While Duffy struggled to remain upright, a black four-door sedan pulled to the curb. It stopped ten feet in front of the staggering Duffy. Two husky men in brown overcoats sprung from the back seat. One took up a position in front of Duffy, the other blocking whatever feeble attempt at retreat the drunk could make.

Duffy tried to step through the wall of muscle blocking his path, but bounced off. The man grabbed his arms, preventing him from crash landing on the sidewalk.

Another individual who rode shotgun got out and leaned against the front fender. He was tall, lean and wore a grey sharkskin suit. The goon supporting Duffy spun him to face the approaching stranger. "This guy's putrid," the man said.

Duffy stared pie-eyed.

"Your name Duffy," the man inquired.

Using the last of his brain's strength, he answered, "A...A...who wants to know?"

The man pulled a leather wallet from his breast pocket. He waved it inches from Duffy's bulbous nose then let the front flap drop.

"Wilcox. Detective Wilcox. Battle Hymn Homicide."
Wilcox acknowledged the two men propping Duffy. "These
giants are my esteemed colleagues."

Duffy mumbled, "What you want with me?"

"You're under arrest," Wilcox said, walking back to the
car.

"You got the wrong guy."

Wilcox whirled around and smirked. "Now that's funny,
mister. I didn't even tell you why we're pickin' you up."

Tongue tied, Duffy managed, "Oh...a ...yeah."

"You're goin' down for Murder One, you drunk."

"Who me?"

"No. Your grandmother."

"Who'd I kill?"

"Don't play dumb. You shot Archie the barber.
Remember him? Put that clown in the back seat, boys."

"Where you takin me," Duffy blubbered.

"Somewhere that has a brand new chair to sit in. We're
anxious to try it out. It's wired to keep your ass nice 'n'
warm."

One of the musclemen hopped in the back. The other
took hold of Duffy's head and steered him to the middle
and jumped in. The car drifted down the street while
Wilcox scanned the faces of pedestrians.

44.

O'Hara broke into a light jog, holding his gun holster against his thigh with one hand, palming the top of his hat with the other.

"I'll kill that no good bastard if what Ron says is true," he said between breaths.

A few minutes later, he stopped at the hospital's front desk, sweat stinging his eyes. The Candy Striper told him Katherine's room number.

"You just missed him," she added.

"Who," O'Hara asked.

"A man who said he was a relative and that he wanted to pay the new mother a visit."

"What'd this guy look like?"

The girl rubbed her temple. "Let me see. He's about your age with black hair."

"Thanks, young lady."

O'Hara used the elevator. When he arrived on the sixth floor, he looked into the nursery. The Kelly bassinette was empty. He quietly made his way to Katherine's room.

* * *

Ron searched the dock. He looked in every spider hole his father might use as a hangover hideaway, and asked other workers if they'd seen him. No luck. He returned to the main gate. The young guard who had confiscated Bob Kelly's knife waved him down.

"Hey. Where's the fire?"

Ron looked at the old trailer. "Is O'Hara in?"

"You mean Officer O'Hara, don't you," the guard corrected.

"I mean my father-in-law."

"Oh. Sorry. I didn't know."

"O'Hara," Ron shouted.

"He's not in there."

"Then where the hell is he?"

The guard pointed toward town. "He went that way."

"Thanks."

Ron continued his pursuit. While doing so, he considered what kind of future there would be for Katherine and the baby if he killed his father then ended up on death row. Instead of town, he retuned to Wood Street and stopped in front of his house. On the front porch, his mother, wrapped in a black shawl, lifted her head.

"Ronnie!" she cried.

He ran to her. "Oh, Ma."

"What is it, son? Why aren't you workin'?"

He looked into her tired eyes. "Something's happened, Ma."

"Is it Katherine?" The baby?"

Ron stroked her wiry hair. "Katherine had the baby."

"Premature!" she gasped. "It isn't, is it?"

"No, Ma. He's as strong as an ox."

"A boy! How wonderful. Mrs. O'Hara was right." Then she asked, "Is it Katherine? Is she?"

"They're both fine." Ron looked in the front window. "Has *he* been here?"

"Not since he left for work this morning. Why?"

Ron patted his mother's cheek. "That's what I want to ask him. Why?"

Perplexed, Mrs. Kelly's looked at her son. "What do ya mean?"

He stooped, took her by the shoulders and kissed her forehead. "I love you, Ma."

She rubbed his forearm. "I know you do, Ronnie. You're a good boy. When can I see the baby? Did you think of a name?"

"Let's give Katherine a day to rest. Then you can see them, okay?"

"Sure, whatever you say, son. Now off you go. You'll be a wonderful father."

Ron gave his mother another peck then headed back to town.

* * *

Katherine had always found confession exhausting. Lying in her hospital bed, she passed in and out of sleep, worried about what would happen next. The squeaky door signaled that a floor nurse had entered the room, poured fresh water in a glass pitcher then left.

In the fog of what had happened, thirst was a difficult concept to wrap her head around. She drifted back to sleep.

Again, the creaking door disturbed her rest. She rubbed her eyes.

"Who is it," she mumbled.

The only response was heavy breathing and pungency. She opened her eyes and there it was, everything years of *"In the Name of the Father, the Son and the Holy Ghost"* had promised to vanquish.

"So, you decided to spill your guts." Kelly displayed his buck knife. The thought of sleep evaporated from Katherine like rain on hot fire. She murmured, "No, Jesus. No." Kelly sheathed his knife and undid his zipper. "This is something you can tell God about."

Her limbs went numb. Kelly snickered, "Remember this?"

He lumbered toward her. The door opened. Katherine screamed, "Daddy!"

Kelly turned to see O'Hara, gun drawn.

"Oh, luck of the Irish," Kelly said, zipping his pants and brimming with glee. "It's the coward and the whore in one room. That'll make it easy."

* * *

The Candy Striper emerged from a nearby office. She carried paperless clipboards and a cup filled with new pencils. "It's you again," she said. "The happy father."

"Yeah, that's me," Ron replied between breaths and running a comb through his messy hair. "The happy father."

"You'd better get up there or you'll miss the party."

"What the heck you talking about?"

"There's two guys up there right now."

"Who," Ron asked, both hands gripping the desk.

"A guy with black hair and a cop. They…"

Ron passed the nursery. He glanced at the baby, who was fast asleep. He walked to Katherine's room. Harsh mumbling caused him to kick the door open. O'Hara's back was to him. Bob Kelly stood between O'Hara and Katherine. O'Hara's gun pointed at Kelly's heart.

Ron didn't know what to do. *Protect Katherine.* He was one electrical impulse away from running to her side, but when he heard the gun hammer click, he noticed six bullets missing from the cartridge loops on O'Hara's holster.

Bob Kelly smiled. "Go ahead, ya coward. Playin' with the empty pea shooter again?" He walked toward O'Hara, his hand extended. "Give me that thing, ya' moron."

O'Hara's finger tightened on the trigger, his body braced for kickback. Kelly made a grab for the weapon.

Without understanding how or why, Ron shouted, "No, Mr. O'Hara, he's not worth it," and lunged forward, grabbing O'Hara's shoulder. The gun discharged and sent Ron and O'Hara crashing to the floor, the pistol sliding across the room

The smell of gunpowder hung in the air. Ron slowly stood.

Bob Kelly pawed at his chest.

"Why'd ya do it to ya father, boy," he whimpered.

"You're no father of mine, you rotten scum," Ron whispered.

Bob Kelly pulled at the buttons of his flannel shirt, exposing a blossom widening on his pale undergarment. His arms fell to his side. He dropped to the floor, and a burgundy pool formed on the linoleum under him. His chest heaved once.

O'Hara remained on the floor, his mouth moving, but nothing spoken. Ron helped him to his feet. O'Hara screamed, "Katherine."

Ron turned to his wife. Blood trickled along the bridge of her nose. The single shot from a double-load shell had passed through Kelly's heart and lodged in her brain.

O'Hara dove for the gun. Ron joined his father-in-law on the floor. They tussled in Kelly's blood until the cop got the better of his son-in-law. O'Hara pressed the barrel to his own temple and pulled the trigger, but Ron jammed his thumb between the hammer and firing pin. O'Hara froze. His lips moved, forming the words, "Katherine, Katherine." Ron yanked the pistol from the catatonic cop's hand.

"There's been enough killing," he shouted.

Seconds later, orderlies, nurses and on-duty physicians burst into the room to find O'Hara in the fetal position, lifeless Bob Kelly inches away, and Ron cradling Katherine.

"I'm so sorry, baby," he sobbed. "I wish you would have told me. I would have protected you." Ron repeated her earlier suggestion; "We could've started a new life somewhere where nobody knows us, you, me and the baby."

45.

"She must be buried in the church cemetery. You must allow it," Mrs. O'Hara pleaded.

"No," said Father Ryan. "She gave up that right when she disobeyed the Church. There is no room for Katherine O'Hara on these scared grounds."

Therefore, on a clear but windy morning in late October, a stunted funeral procession made its way to the potter's cemetery.

The funeral director drove the hearse while Mrs. O'Hara and Ron joined him in the front seat. The baby remained at home with Mrs. Kelly. The lone civilian vehicle was the Ford station wagon containing Joe Geary and three young steel mill guards.

As the procession stopped on the road near the northernmost section of the rocky cemetery, the sun went behind a cluster of clouds that swept over Blue Mountain. Ron and Mrs. O'Hara walked arm-in-arm as they took their places graveside. Geary and the three guards joined the funeral director at the back of the hearse.

The director commented, "Though this is a small coffin, I'm not sure the four of you will be able to lift it and see the poor girl to her resting place."

Geary's expression hardened.

"Two of you guards take a handle on either side. The third will steer from behind. Leave the rest to me."

The director opened the tailgate and Geary clasped both arms around the top of the simple wooden casket. With three-quarters of the coffin exposed, two guards took hold of brass handles. At the edge of the bumper, the guard, who had frequently spoken with Mr. O'Hara, manned the tail end.

Geary led the procession over rough terrain. When they arrived at Katherine's grave, the coffin was placed on top of planks of wood and two heavy ropes. The pallbearers stood across from Ron and Mrs. O'Hara, who openly wept.

Ron pulled her to his side, and whispered, "Why?"

The funeral director served as chaplain. He stood at the foot of the grave, swallowing nervously. He held a sheet of paper in his hand, information about Katherine garnered from an article that had been published in the *Battle Hymn Hearth*. When he finished his speech, only the blustering wind sang a mournful refrain.

Ron placed a handful of dirt on top of the coffin. From her coat pocket, Mrs. O'Hara produced a palm-size crucifix and stuck it in the soil at the head of the grave. "That's Katherine's cross," she said. "It was tacked to the wall above her bed."

The director began to lead them to the waiting hearse, but Ron stopped at a burial plot in the row next to Katherine's. Mrs. O'Hara held his hand.

"Take good care of her, Isaac," he said. "She'll need a guide."

* * *

Geary watched as the hearse left the cemetery. "Lets do this," he said.

He and one of the guards took hold of the ropes. They carefully lifted the casket and placed it to the side. They removed the wood and lowered Katherine into the dark, stony earth. Two cemetery attendants with shovels in hand stood at the ready near a mound of dirt.

"Be gentle," Geary warned the gravediggers, wiping his eyes.

Geary drove the station wagon down the stone road, turned onto the highway and sped back to town.

* * *

Mrs. Kelly was on the front porch when the hearse dropped Ron and Mrs. O'Hara at the curb.

"You're coming in, aren't you, Mrs. O Hara," Ron asked. "Don't you want to see the baby?"

Mrs. O'Hara waved to Mrs. Kelly who took hold of the infant's arm and waved back.

"There's grandma, sweetie," Mrs. Kelly said, returning into the house.

"No, Ron," Mrs. O'Hara said. "I don't have the strength. Maybe in a few weeks." She looked toward town. "I've got to change my clothes and get back to the hospital." She began to weep. "They, they still can't get John to speak or eat. He just lays in bed."

Ron embraced her as he would his own mother.

"I love you, Mrs. O'Hara."

"If it was thirty or forty years from now," she sniffled, "you kids might have made it."

"I don't know," Ron replied. "I can't think about the future. I've gotta deal with today."

She hugged him and walked solemnly across Division Avenue onto the Catholic section of Wood Street.

* * *

In need of solitude, Ron stayed at Geary's, waiting for the second half of his exam. The baby remained with Mrs. Kelly. Almost a month later, after passing the test and before departing Geary's for the last time, he sat in the private booth and drank coffee. He waved to Lenny and Lenny gave him the thumbs up.

He walked to the register and slid a quarter across the counter.

"Your money's not worth a hill of beans in this place," Geary said, sending the coin on its return trip.

A cab took Ron to Wood Street where his mother waited. There was a suitcase beside her, a tiny valise slung over her shoulder and the wiggling infant in her arms.

"Wait here," Ron told the cabbie. "I'll be right back."

"Okay, kid. But the meter's runnin'."

Ron vaulted to the porch, carried the luggage to the cab and tossed it in the trunk.

Mrs. Kelly walked carefully, cooing in response to the infant's babble. She passed the baby to her son. Magee peered through her curtain. Mrs. Kelly smiled and waved goodbye.

"Where to now," the cabby asked.

"Greyhound bus station," Mrs. Kelly said.

"Gotcha," replied the driver.

Traffic was light on that day in late November. Ron looked out the window as they moved along the main drag, past Gerber's and Archie's boarded up barbershop. "Driver, wait," he said.

The cabbie came to a quick stop on the side of the road. "What'd ya forget, kid?"

"I have to make a stop before we go to the bus station." Mrs. Kelly looked puzzled.

"Fine with me," the cabby chuckled. "Money's money. Where to?"

The baby giggled at who knows what.

"Toony's Hardware," Ron said. "It's in the old part of town."

"You don't have to tell me about that place, buddy. It's a real tourist attraction ever since they charged that Duffy guy with murder. He'll probably get the chair for killin' the barber. Tough luck for him, but good luck for me. People wanna see where the whole thing started. They won't walk there, but a comfy cab ride does the trick."

The driver put the car in gear. A few minutes later, it came to a stop in front of Toony's.

"Here we are, darkie central."

Ron's body tightened. His mother took hold of his arm. "Son..."

"Give me the boy, Ma. I'll be right back."

The driver laughed. "I get it. You're goin' to get an autograph or a picture with the baby. Smart. It'll make a nice gift when he grows up."

The baby's cooing shoved Ron's anger aside. He climbed the two flights of stairs and tapped on the door.

"Who is it," came the exhausted response.

"It's Ron, Mr. Toony." The door opened. "I remembered that you got out of jail yesterday. I wanted to see you before we leave town."

Ben looked tired, old, but not defeated.

"Son," he said. "It's so good to see you."

Ron grinned, shifting the baby to his other arm.

"It's good to see you, too, Ben. I want you to meet someone."

Martha's curiosity got the best of her, drawing her from the back of the flat.

"Ah, the baby," Ben said. His voice thinned. "I'm so sorry about what happened to Katherine."

"Ma, me and the baby are movin' on," Ron said. "There's no life for us here."

Martha stood behind her husband, fixated on the infant.

"Wanna hold him," Ron asked.

She walked around Ben and stood on the landing.

"I sure would," she whispered.

Ron passed her the little boy.

"Here you go, Mrs. Toony."

She brought the child to her breast and kissed his head.

"Oh, he's wonderful."

The baby burped and squeezed Martha's little finger.

"He's my boy," Ron replied.

"Yes, he is," Ben added.

"What's his name," Martha asked.

"Well," Ron began, "me and Katherine talked about it for a long time. After a lot of back and forth, she decided that if our kid was a boy, we'd name him Isaac."

"Isaac, how wonderful," she replied, holding back tears.

Ben rubbed the baby's head of black hair.

"What are you goin' to do?"

"Like I told you, we're leaving Battle Hymn. This kid needs to be raised in a new town. Someplace where nobody knows anything about him."

Ben nodded. "I understand."

"What about you," Ron inquired. "You stayin' here?"

"Well," Ben said. "Tom Davis died and his wife offered me and Martha to come and run her store in Alabama. We thought long and hard on it, but our place is here. We've gotta carry on for our boy." He pinched his brow. "That's all there is to live for."

Martha passed the baby to Ron.

"I'll make sure this boy understands how he got his name and what it means," Ron assured them.

Ben rested his hand on Ron's shoulder. "You'll let us know when you're settled?"

"I've got my electrician's license and that'll help me get a job," Ron replied. "I just gotta find another steel town."

"You will, boy. You will."

Each blinked and touched the other's arms.

"Gotta go, Ben."

"Write and tell us about Isaac's life."

"Will do."

Ben closed the door. Martha wailed.

Ron got in the cab and passed Isaac to Mrs. Kelly.

"Let's go the bus station," he said.

"On my way," the driver replied, clicking his tongue to the beat of the meter.

EPILOGUE

Mrs. Kelly, in an aisle seat, nuzzled the child. The baby hadn't fussed or whined since he'd left the hospital a month earlier. Overhead, the suitcase banged around as the bus pulled away from the depot. Before the vehicle entered the brand new section of the PA Turnpike, it passed the city morgue. Inside, a box containing Bob Kelly's ashes gathered dust on a metal shelf in a closet.

The driver revved the engine after getting his toll card.

"I hear someday they're gonna make a tunnel that goes right through this blasted hill," Mrs. Kelly commented as the bus started toward Blue Mountain and up the only road out of the valley.

"They already did," said Ron. "We'll be there in a few minutes."

Ron's lips drew a sliver of a smile as he stared at the backdrop of his fading youth – the river, the woods and the hills. But what snared his attention was the blinking red light on the smokestack of blast furnace "C", and the sprawling steel mill. For him, these were memories. He'd have to grow new roots in another town. There, he could make a home for his half-brother and the boy's stepmother.

From the baby's valise, Mrs. Kelly pulled a recent copy of the *Hearth*.

"Here," she said, offering the front page, "I brought this along for the ride. It'll help keep your mind off things."

"Thanks, Ma," said Ron. He flattened the paper on his lap. *"Unseasonably cool,"* read the weather report. *"Military Advisers move into more active roles in the tiny country of Vietnam, "* read another. The headline splashed in black read,

**PRESIDENT AND FIRST LADY BEGIN
THREE-DAY SWING THROUGH TEXAS.**

Below the type was a stock photo of the president, Mrs. Kennedy and their two children, Caroline and John-John. Mrs. Kelly tapped the page. "You think we've got it tough? That man has the whole world on his shoulders."

Ron rubbed the baby's chin, rested his own head on the window, and absorbed the irregular roadway as the bus struggled through its eighteen gears. Halfway up the hill it passed a large black and white sign.

**YOU ARE LEAVING BATTLE HYMN
STEEL TOWN, U.S.A.**

www.ingramcontent.com/pod-product-compliance
Lightning Source LLC
Chambersburg PA
CBHW060129130626
46556CB00006B/2283